Dead
Inside

Chandler Morrison

DEATH'S HEAD PRESS

an imprint of Dead Sky Publishing, LLC
Miami Beach, Florida
www.deadskypublishing.com

ISBN: 9781639510528

First Edition

Cover Art: Daniella Batsheva

Book Layout: Lori Michelle
www.TheAuthorsAlley.com

For Jeff Burk

"The death, then, of a beautiful woman is, unquestionably, the most poetical topic in the world."

—Edgar Allan Poe

T oo warm.
Too wet.

Too alive.

That's how I would describe her mouth.

She gets up from between my legs and wipes the back of her hand across her pouty lips, looking at me with an expression I can't decipher—I've never been all that great at reading people—but I know it's indicative of something less than positive.

"Sorry," I say, because she looks like she wants me to say something. "It's not happening."

"*Clearly*," she says, raising an eyebrow, her mouth turned down. "God, what's *wrong* with you?" Her lipstick is badly smeared, and I think about telling her, but the tone of her voice seems pointed, maybe even angry, so I let it go.

"What do you mean," I ask, my own voice sounding blander than I'd intended, but I've never been all that great at expressing myself, either. I don't even know what I'm *supposed* to express right now. She's buttoning her blouse, and all I can think about is how silly it was of her to unbutton it in the first place; the little "favor" she'd tried to perform didn't require any nakedness on her part. Showing off, perhaps? Her breasts are decent, but not spectacular, and she didn't take off her bra, so there wasn't much

7

to show, anyway. Even if she had, would it have made a difference? Turned me on, so to speak? I doubt it. That had been the point of this whole experiment: to see if anything had changed.

I really don't think anything ever changes.

I don't *want* anything to change.

Her offer had seemed like an easy opportunity to test the waters again, but it's always the same . . . weird, tense, and unnatural. I just want her to leave.

"How are you not even *hard*?" she asks, her voice still jagged with that spiteful sourness. "I've been sucking on that thing for, like, fifteen fucking *minutes*. If *that* didn't get you hard . . . I mean, Jesus."

I think she's offended. I've called into question her abilities as a woman. Hell hath no fury. If only she knew what she'd just had her mouth on. If only she knew where it had been.

This must be my cue to say something, because she's looking at me silently. "Um . . . do you want . . . some water," I ask. I have no intention of getting her any water.

She shakes her head, biting her lip and glaring at me. "That's all you have to say? *Really*?"

I hate dealing with women. They can't be up front about anything.

Amend that. I hate dealing with *people*. They can't be up front about anything. Please don't confuse my misanthropy for misogyny.

"Jesus," she says again, grabbing her purse and glancing at her phone. "You know, I appreciate you getting me through Biochem this semester. Really, I do. But *seriously*, there have been guys who have done a lot more for me and gotten a lot less, so when

I offer you a blowjob just because you let me copy your fucking homework—"

It was actually a lot more than that; I'd been her lab partner, "partner" used very loosely because I did *everything* while she stood around doing whatever the hell it is that brainless college girls do. And I did it not out of the expectance of sexual favors, but simply because we were graded as a pair, not as individuals. I never gave a fuck about her. I just wanted the A.

"—the *least* you could do is pretend to *enjoy* it. I give *damn* good head, so if you didn't get anything out of that, you're either gay or, or . . . I don't know, *not right*."

Gay? No, not my speed. Not right, though? That sounds about right. By conventional definitions of the word, at least, and convention has always irked me just enough to shy away from it whenever possible. You can't put a label on me. You wouldn't want to.

"You skinny little four-eyed *freak*," she spits, her cheeks blooming crimson with anger. People get so upset about the strangest things. Overreaction—it's the American way. It's . . . *conventional*. "Are you high, or something? What the fuck is *wrong* with you? That blank look on your face hasn't changed since I got here. I don't think it's changed during the whole semester, actually. You always look like such a fucking zombie."

"Listen," I say, looking at my watch, a purely-for-show gesture since I already know what time it is, *always* know what time it is. "I have to get to work. You should probably go."

"It's ten thirty at night. If you want me out, you could at least come up with a better excuse than *that*."

"Graveyard shift. Security guard at Preston Druse Charity Hospital. I've told you that at least half a dozen times this semester." I'm not sure if that's true or not, because I avoided conversation with the dumb cunt as much as possible, but it doesn't matter, either way. I *do* need to get to work, and her perfume is starting to make me nauseous. I'm totally regretting this whole experiment.

"You really are a prick," she says, tossing her hair over her shoulder and putting her hand on her hip, probably not realizing how ridiculous it makes her look. That aside, though, I look at her and realize she *is* pretty, at least conventionally so, and most heterosexual males would kill to have her on her knees in their bedroom. Still, there's just . . . too much color in her face, too much light in her eyes . . . and I can *feel* the warm body heat radiating off her. I imagine her colder, paler. She could be almost perfect, if she wasn't oozing all that spritely vitality. There is no greater tragedy than beauty needlessly wasted.

"Stop *looking* at me like that. You're creeping me out."

Annoyed, I bite the inside of my cheek and take off my glasses, polishing the lenses with the cuff of my sleeve. "I think you should go," I say again.

She stands there a moment longer, then mutters something under her breath, turns on her heel, and marches out. I watch her legs as she goes, thighs muscular and pliable, moving lithely under her short skirt. I picture them atrophied and slightly wrinkled, spiderwebbed with purple veins against a backdrop of icy flesh, white and smooth as marble.

As I dress myself for work, I'm daydreaming of chilly kisses punctuated with black tongues and chipped, gray teeth.

The hospital is quiet at night. Television gives the impression that large medical facilities are always bustling with frantic activity. That's either a blatant untruth, concocted for the sake of dramatic set pieces, or Preston Druse Charity Hospital is an anomaly to which that particular rule does not apply. I don't know. I don't care. All I care about is the fact that *this* hospital, come nightfall, lowers its voice to a hushed murmur, permeated by the barely noticeable chirps of uncaring vitality monitors, the sparse staff's whispered conversations, and the occasional steady sighs of a breathing machine. The halls are all but empty, excepting a few nurses' stations and, sometimes, a skulking doctor frowning down at a clipboard.

People rarely attempt to engage me. Maybe it's because everyone is busy, but it's probably because of my general demeanor, which in the past and present has been described as "unapproachable" and "creepy". Even the janitor, a pleasant and friendly old war veteran who seems to be well-liked by all, usually avoids me as one would avoid a nest of wasps. One that appears to be vacant but could possibly erupt into a violent swarm of insects at any moment.

It is no matter. I prefer the level of invisibility I am afforded here. In the three years of my employment at this establishment, never have my services actually been required—no escaped mental patients, no intruders, no suspicious activity—so I sit in the tiny security room reading Poe and Bukowski, glancing every now and again at the camera monitors and making periodic, uneventful rounds through the building. I am a mere formality, a small blip on the payroll, and a largely unnoticed presence about the premises.

This is exactly the way I like it. I am a harmless phantom, floating below the radar of perception, granting me a ghostly existence that permits me to freely engage in my unusual extracurriculars.

People don't see me, and I don't really see them.

It's better for everyone that way.

The nearly dead have a certain scent about them. In a weak attempt at socialization, I once made the mistake of divulging this lovely tidbit of information to a college classmate after I'd been working at the hospital for a year or so.

The conversation had taken place in a poetry workshop, if my memory serves true, and my colleague was already visibly unnerved by my slightly satanic sonnet. When I made the offhand comment about the smell of the dying, he shifted uncomfortably in his seat and picked at his thumbnail. "Yeah?" he said. "Um, what do they . . . smell like?"

I could tell he really didn't want to know the answer to that question; he was clearly trying to be polite in case I was some murderous Columbine wannabe who kept track of anyone exhibiting the faintest amounts of disrespect, but it was too late for me to back out of the conversation. Making a mental note to, in the future, avoid such topics with ordinary citizens, I said, "They smell like . . . like a kind of slipping away, I guess. Like something that's there but is noticeably fading. Like the last whiffs of a dream. It's . . . a stale smell." I paused, but I could tell the poor bloke was becoming more and more freaked out, so I figured I might as well deliver a finishing blow. "I love it," I'd said, staring coldly at him. "I love it almost as much as I love the smell of the recently dead."

"Listen, I need to get going," he'd said, gathering his things in sloppy haste. "Uh, great poem, nice talking to you, see you next week." He'd almost tripped over his own feet on the way out the door. The professor had watched him go and then turned her gaze to me, raising an eyebrow. I'd just shrugged.

Yes, the *smell*.

The *slipping away*.

I can smell it tonight.

It hits me while I'm making my rounds through the recovery ward, strolling down the wide hallway with my hands in my pockets, whistling a low tune, something I think the Reaper would whistle if *he* were the one walking down the hall. Maybe it is.

The smell wafts thickly, in a cloud almost visible, out from a room across from a storage closet, a mop bucket sitting in forgotten solitude near the doorway. This leads me to assume that everyone's favorite janitor is keeping the occupant company—something he's known to do—performing magic tricks or telling lewd jokes. A candy striper *and* a toilet scrubber, all in one. Only the finest get to work at the thirty-sixth-best hospital in Ohio. It's a treasure trove of talent.

See, even creeps like me can have a sense of humor.

That *was* humor, right? Like, sarcasm? I don't know, you get what I'm saying.

When I peek in the small room, which reeks deliciously of impending death, the comedic custodian is nowhere to be seen. With a quick glance over my shoulder to make sure no one is coming, I slip inside and stare down at the person lying on the narrow bed, tucked neatly into starched white sheets, so still and peaceful. It's a female, though this is discernible only from the slight frame and the moderately large breasts hidden beneath the pale blue hospital gown; her entire head, save for the bruised and blackened left eye, is shrouded in gauze polka-dotted with blooms of deep crimson. Her right arm is encased in a cast, and the left one has been amputated at the elbow. I look at her chart, attached to a clipboard dangling from the side of the bed on a length of string. Abigail M. Turpentine, age twenty-eight. Boating accident. Severe internal bleeding, cerebral hemorrhaging, more than thirty bone fractures, and a handful of severed arteries. Surgery had taken place less than three hours ago, and if the death smell is any indication, it hadn't been entirely successful.

Keeping an eye on the vital signs, which for the time being are steady, I say to her in a hushed tone, "A boating accident. You don't hear about those too often. Beats a boring old car crash or heart attack, I suppose." She doesn't stir, and her one visible eye remains firmly shut. "I bet you look pretty awful under all those bandages," I whisper, trying to picture it. "Like somebody took a weed-whacker to your face. Or a . . . cheese grater." I touch my fingers to her neck, feeling the faint pulse. Her flesh is still too warm. "The coldness is coming. And even with your fucked-up face—especially with your fucked-up face—you'll still be beautiful to me."

I'm feeling good as I take the elevator back down to the lobby. Usually I just go down to the morgue and see what I can find, relying on the luck of the draw, but every once in a while, I'll be confronted with that smell, and I'll know what's in store for me. Abigail M. Turpentine will flatline soon, almost certainly before my next shift. Sure, it'll be a great and terrible tragedy for the friends and family and whatever—sound Taps and usher in the Greek chorus—but hey, I have needs, too.

Now, make no mistake, I have no delusions of sanity; I consider myself to be vastly intelligent and egregiously well-read, and anyone with *half* of a functioning intellect would know that a person with my proclivities is a few shades of fucked up. Self-awareness really doesn't mean shit, though. It is, in fact, little more than psychological masturbation, and has about the same net worth as a wad of semen in a handful of crumpled tissues. No cockroach ever desired *not* to be a cockroach, just because it knew it was a cockroach.

Besides, there are far worse things I could be doing; I'd be willing to stake a reasonable amount of money on the hypothesis that my former lab partner probably does more of those things on a Thursday night than I'll ever do in the entirety of my life. Guilt really doesn't factor into this particular equation.

Before returning to the quiet solitude of my post in the security room, I step outside under the awning of the main entrance and fire up a Lucky Strike. I breathe in the sweet summer air with the deliciously toxic cloud of carcinogenic pollutants, gazing out at the mostly empty parking lot and thinking about Abigail M. Turpentine, age twenty-eight, boating accident. Head wrapped up like a Christmas present that might as well be addressed to yours truly. I'm smiling as I let the smoke out of my lungs and into the warm July night.

In my mind, I'm already unwrapping the bandages.

Christmas in July, indeed.

I'm still thinking about it as I make my rounds the following night. I feel giddy, with the anticipation a normal male would have had for a girl as traditionally attractive as my lab partner, if she had made it clear how she intended to express her gratitude. Ms. Turpentine was not in her room when I checked earlier this evening—an elderly dog-attack victim had taken her place—and since I very much doubt she's been discharged with a prescription for mild narcotics and orders to "get plenty of rest and drink lots of fluids", I think it's safe to assume she's taken up residence in the basement morgue.

The last stop on my patrol, before I head down to the land of recently dead, is the maternity ward, an irony that does not escape me.

It stands to be said that I hate babies, therefore I hate the maternity ward. There's something about the creation of life that really pisses me off, not to mention the fact that they're gross and needy and all they do is eat and shit and cry and sleep. I'm really not a violent creature by nature, but there's nothing like a wailing infant to drive me to the brink of contemplating homicide. I once expressed my hatred of babies to one of the many psychiatrists my mother made me see, and he'd nodded and written something down and said, "Yes, yes, well then. Have you considered that babies are still *people*, just smaller and less developed? Tell me, at what age do people stop being so bothersome to you?"

"They don't," I'd said. Which is true; *all* people are bothersome to me, I can relate to none of them, but at least adults don't (for the most part, at least) shit their pants and scream bloody murder when they don't get what they want. I've never been any kind of athlete or anything, but am I *seriously* the *only* person who realizes that infants are the *perfect* punting shape? If we replaced footballs with babies, I would have been far more successful in high school gym class.

My hands are trembling at my sides as I stand looking down at the sheet-covered corpse on the silver metal slab. The pale, name-tagged feet stick out at the end, toenails sexily yellowed by the throes of putrid rot. I run the tips of my quivering fingers up and down the soles of her feet, the flesh rough and hard, like calluses.

Not taking my eyes off the obscured figure before me, I step around the side of the slab to stand by her head, eager to throw back the sheet but forcing myself to have restraint, willing patience into muscles twitching with anticipation. I want to savor this. The painfully boring blowjob has stirred up a thrumming lust in my loins, and it's been weeks since I've taken a dead lover.

I pull the sheet back with my tremor-wrought hand, stopping at her neck, revealing the girl's face. The bandages have been removed, which is a disappointment, as I would very much have liked to have done that myself, but people with affectations like mine can't really afford to be choosy.

The boating accident really did a number on her features, and if not for the womanliness visible underneath the sheet, her sex would be otherwise indecipherable. The surgeons have shaved her head, and without hair to draw attention away from her face, the wounds upon it are ghastlier—*deliciously* so. Patches of her skin are pink and wrinkled, as the result of savage burns, and there are chunks of it missing completely, the edges of the gashes torn and jagged, making them look like an animal had taken large bites out of her face. The biggest hole is in her right cheek, revealing rows of pearlescent teeth set in pale gums. Her nose is gone, as is her right eye, and a long, curved abrasion along her scalp reveals the white of her skull. I touch the back of my hand to her cool forehead, as if checking for a fever, and the sensation of her dead skin sends chills down my already-shivering spine.

I peel away the rest of the sheet with painstaking

slowness, letting it crumple to the floor, leaving her naked, exposed in all of her lifeless glory. Her body isn't as mangled as her face, but the injuries that are present are each uniquely beautiful in their own right. Her plump breasts are mostly intact, save a few minor lesions and a missing nipple. Her stomach, flat two nights ago but now bloated with corpse gas, has a number of lesions and small lacerations, and her thighs and calves are marked by crisscrossed cuts and scrapes. I return to the foot of the slab and spread her long, stiff legs, revealing a closely-shaved pubic region and a vagina that graciously appears to be unharmed.

My erection is pulsing so fiercely within my pants that it's almost painful.

"I'm certain you were an object of much desire among living men," I say to her, gently caressing her calf. Talking to dead girls has always been easier for me than talking to live ones, allowing for a kind of poetic eloquence that is otherwise unavailable to me. "Maybe you were even kind of promiscuous. I can see you on that boat, flirting with the boys and teasing them with your . . . *assets*." I frown, thinking about the young men who surely drooled after her like dogs, and I say, "I hope they died, too. I hope it was painful for them. They wouldn't be interested in you now, anyway. They've had their turn with you, ogling your body, so filled with warmth and blood and life, fucking you and ejaculating to the lively sounds of your orgasms." I light a cigarette, casting a smirking glance at the "NO SMOKING" sign; there aren't any smoke detectors down here (or security cameras, for that matter), and there's nothing like pre- and post-coital cigarettes.

"Yes, I bet you wailed when they fucked you, and I bet they loved it. Frankly, I've never understood why men are so enamored by that. Female orgasm has never interested me. Probably because you have to be alive to have an orgasm." I make a sound that's sort of, *almost*, like laughter—more like a sickly gag, I guess—and cough on the smoke that catches in my throat. "Their time with you is over now, though, and it's my turn. You'd scream if you could, out of pleasure or fear, I do not know. Maybe they're one and the same."

I can't take it much longer. Her body calls to me, pleading to be violated, and the moment to comply has come. I stub my cigarette out and put it in my back pocket before commencing the ritualistic stages of undress—first the shoes, then the pants, the tie, the shirt, and lastly the underwear, freeing my throbbing penis into the cold, still air.

"Get ready," I whisper to her, my voice quavering. I feel like all the blood in my body has rushed into my groin, and there's an undeniable magnetism between our genitalia, pulling me toward her, beckoning me into her. I spread her legs a little wider and mount her, groaning as I slide myself into the cold dryness of her unlubricated vaginal canal. Gripping the sides of the icy metal table, eyes crawling over her gorgeously ravaged body, I begin to thrust.

Okay, before I go on, I should warn you that this next part is what most people would consider to be *gross* or *appalling*. If you were expecting fifty shades of softcore mommy porn, you're going to be disappointed.

Consider this your goddamn trigger warning.

So, I'm thrusting. I always start slow, no matter how strong the urge in my loins, pushing myself into her as far as I can go and then pausing mid-thrust, holding it there, body trembling, before pulling back until just the tip resides within her, at which point I push forward once again, the loud *clap!* sound of our genitals slamming into each other sending bursts of ecstasy into my brain.

I moan, quickening my pace a little. I shift my inconsiderable weight to my right arm so I can run my left hand over her upper body, squeezing her full, firm breasts and slipping my thumb into the hole where her right nipple should be. I press on her bloated belly, causing an eruption of gas to escape loudly from her mouth and anus, the scent at once arresting my sinuses with sweet pungency. Leaning down, I kiss her mangled lips, tasting the acrid remnants of the death breath still slithering up from her esophagus. When I again push on her stomach, she belches once more, sour fumes filling my mouth and surging down my throat—I can even feel a cool puff of air shoot from her vagina, which is beginning to tear and chafe with the friction of my now-frenzied movements.

I think this is the part where two living people would achieve the peak feeling of bodily conjunction, their carnal union at its explosive conclusion. I've heard of simultaneous orgasm—that's usually how it happens in the movies, anyway—but I'm unsure of how often it actually occurs, if at all. The two living girls I've been with never came at all, and my own "climax" was nothing memorable, the faint pleasure paling in comparison to the ecstasy I feel when I ejaculate into a dead woman. The dead have no expectations; there's no pressure for you to make them feel anything. I copulate with corpses largely because it is all about *me*, about the meeting of *my* needs—my dead sexual partners exist only to bring *me* pleasure, and they require nothing in return.

I bury my face in her neck, so as to muffle my baboon-like hooting as I stab my pelvis forward for one final thrust, shooting thousands of doomed children in the general direction of her dead and useless ovaries. Another benefit of my little fetish— no condom, no problem. I could very well be the most fertile man on the planet, but my lovers are all equipped with the best birth control the world can offer. As in, dead reproductive systems. I know that goes without saying, but I like to say it. Dead eggs. Barren uteruses. Fruitless wombs.

I collapse off her and land on my side on the cold metal floor, hurting my ribs, but the pain is flushed away by the residual euphoria that's flooding my body. My groin is still pulsating with swirling warmth, and my abdominal muscles are flexing achingly, *ecstatically*. My entire physical being has been restored with glimmering life, all thanks to the delights of a girl filled with abyssal death. Her void fills my own.

I roll over and crawl to my pile of clothes, pawing through them and digging in my pants pocket for my cigarettes and lighter. I fire one up and lie back down on the floor, breathing heavily, sweat glistening on my skin in spite of the chilled air. "Goddamn," I say, letting smoke out of my nostrils. "I haven't had a lay like that in months. You have my deepest gratitude,

Ms. Turpentine. Just think, our lovemaking has given purpose and significance to your death. A tragic boating accident that leaves a young girl dead is one thing, but it becomes something else entirely when your lifeless body contributes to a union more fervently passionate than that which any living person could ever try to replicate. I will not forget this night."

The following week, still satisfied from my tryst with Abigail, I'm dozing in the security room when the radio on my belt squawks and a panicked female voice shouts, *"Security! Security! We've got a situation in room 13B, you need to get here, NOW!"*

I rub my eyes and sit up, yawning. Taking the radio off my belt, I say, "What do you mean you have a situation. What kind of situation."

A long pause, then, *"JUST GET THE FUCK UP HERE!"* It sounds like there's screaming in the background.

I breathe a groaning sigh and then say, "All right. I'm coming now." I get up and leave the little office to head for the elevator, thinking I should have checked the security feed for that room before going so I could have an idea what I was up against. We don't *have* "situations" at this hospital. I assume the nurse is new, probably an intern or a medical student, and is freaking out about something minor. It's four in the morning at Preston Druse Hospital; what could possibly be going on that's important enough to involve the otherwise-unneeded security guard?

Room 13B is in the maternity ward. As I've said

before, I hate this part of the hospital, so in accordance with Murphy's Law, *of course* this would be the location of the mystery "situation". Whatever it is, no matter how bad, I'm not touching any fucking babies. I didn't sign up for that shit.

As I proceed down the hall toward the room in question, I hear a male voice scream, *"SHE CAN'T BE DEAD! SHE CAN'T BE FUCKING DEAD!"*

I quicken my step a little, figuring that a woman had died in childbirth, and now the husband is getting belligerent. Christ, people are so goddamn sensitive.

When I step inside 13B, several things are immediately apparent.

First, is that the mother has, in fact, *not* died in childbirth; she's lying in the bed, sobbing, holding a newborn to her chest, naked and with the umbilical cord still attached. It isn't crying, its limbs are sprawled out limply, and its skin is a cool bluish color. I don't know much about babies, but I know they're technically not supposed to be blue.

Next is that the screaming man, presumably the father, is barely being restrained by three nurses who are fighting to get him under control as he bucks and thrashes against their grips, shrieking and yowling like a house cat that's gotten caught in a bear trap. His sweaty hair hangs in his face, which blushes cherry-red with fury. One of the nurses has a busted lip and a bleeding nose, bent at an awkward angle.

The final thing I notice is the doctor, a pretty woman with thick glasses and blonde hair tied back in a ponytail, her attractiveness marred only by the fact that she isn't dead. She's standing in the corner, seemingly removed from all the chaos, staring at the woman in the bed. She has eyes like halogen lamps, but there's something strange about them, like the light in them is cold and detached. They're glossed-over and hazy, cast with a beautiful *deadness* that I'm used to seeing when I peel back the eyelids of my lovers. There's something else in them, too, though ... there's a *hunger* that emits not only from her eyes, but haunts her entire face, and it's then that I realize she *isn't* staring at the woman in the bed—she's staring at the dead baby in the woman's arms.

"*Hello?*" one of the nurses, the one with the bludgeoned face, shouts at me. "*Fucking DO SOMETHING!*"

This really isn't my area of expertise. My figure is lanky and spindly, and not designed for physical confrontation. I've never been in a fight, I'm not sure I even know how to throw a punch. The thumb gets tucked inside the fist, right? Or is it the other way around?

I don't have time to think about it, though, because the man breaks free from the nurses and barrels past me, knocking me onto the floor. He snatches something shiny and silver from a pushcart filled with medical supplies, and then charges over to the woman in the bed, shouting, "*Don't worry, honey, we're gonna go see her now!*" He raises the silver object—which I now realize is a scalpel—over his head, and plunges it into the woman's breast. Blood splatters onto his face and chest. The woman screams in horror and pain, but only for a moment, because the man withdraws the blade and jabs it deep into her eye, abruptly cutting her off. All the nurses are screaming now, and I can hear commotion coming from the hall as more personnel flock to the scene. The doctor, though, remains silently rooted in place, still staring at the infant with that ravenous look in her eyes.

"FUCK ALL OF YOU!" the man bellows at us as he wrenches the scalpel free from his dead wife's skull. *"YOU LET HER DIE!"* There are tears streaming down his stubbly cheeks and plunking onto the collar of his wrinkled, bloodstained shirt. If ever there existed true grief in its purest form, it is within this man. He drags the blade across his throat, spraying freshets of dark gore onto the bed and linoleum. The nurses' screams increase in volume. The doctor keeps staring.

Someone calls the police, and they come and ask us all kinds of silly questions, in their silly officious voices, while we stand in the hallway. The crime scene unit takes pictures of the mess in the labor room, now sanctioned off by yellow DO NOT CROSS tape. I've been watching the doctor the whole time; she seems distracted and dazed, which I suppose could be from shock, but I don't think it is. There's something about her that isn't quite right. Her eyes, though—those big, dead eyes—they're mesmerizing. Her irises are like hard blue ice encased in dusty crystalline globes, glimpses of Neptune through a telescope with a breath-fogged lens.

In listening to her talk to the cop with the notebook, I learn she is Helen Winchester, head maternity doctor here at the hospital. She works mostly after-hours, but if there's a reason for this—and I suspect there must be—she doesn't provide it.

It disturbs me how much I'm drawn to her. Maybe it's the eyes, or that air of off-ness about her. I can't quite call it attraction, though she *is* attractive by all the standards otherwise foreign to me, and if she were dead, I wouldn't be able to get my pants off fast enough. But she's *not* dead, even if her eyes indicate differently, so she shouldn't be of any interest to me.

While the cop is questioning her, she catches me staring at her. Unable to look away, transfixed by the spell of her eyes, I hold her gaze for a few long moments. A chill runs down my spine, a shiver as cold as the murky blue orbs behind her glasses. It's as though she's looking *into* me, like she can see me for the perverse freak I am, but instead of turning away in disgust, she seems almost captivated. I suppose it's something that could be a trick of the light, or a misinterpretation of the cool stillness floating around her pupils, but I doubt it. When I can no longer hold her stare, I walk off down the hallway. The director of the hospital gave the rest of the night off to all those present at the scene of the crime, so I leave and drive home. It's cold within my car, despite the warm summer night, and I can almost feel Helen's presence, as though she were in the back seat, boring holes in my head with the frosty flame of her gaze.

Something has been set in motion. I don't know what it is, or how I know it, but I am afraid.

The next night I follow her on the camera monitors, watching her go from room to room, patient to patient, her movements gentle and lithe, her face smiling when she's talking to people, but solemn and downcast when she's alone between conversations. There's no audio on the cameras, so I don't know what she's saying, but I suspect her voice is as it was the night prior: light and pleasant, but subdued and almost overly calm, making one wonder if she's naturally of a mellow temperament, or if she just doesn't give a fuck about the people around her, or what they have to say. I hope it's the latter.

Her rounds throughout the hospital are uneventful and boring, so I allow myself to doze a few times in my chair before waking to track her down again by flipping through the monitors. This goes on for the first three hours of my shift until she hangs her long white coat in her office, takes a blue duffel bag from underneath her desk, and walks to the elevator. I switch to the elevator camera and watch as she bushes the "B" button for the basement.

Now, the only place of any real note in the basement is . . . the morgue. There are a couple of supply rooms, but they don't contain anything a maternity doctor should need, and certainly not at the end of her shift. Why, though, would said maternity doctor need anything from the morgue?

I think of the way she looked at that dead baby last night. I try to make something of it, try to come up with some sort of explanation, but am unable to draw any conclusions, logical or otherwise.

And yet, here she is, swiping her keycard and entering the Cold Room of the Corpses.

For the first time, I am distraught by the fact that there aren't any cameras in the morgue.

I swivel in my chair with my fingers steepled, clucking my tongue and thinking about how best to proceed. There's probably a perfectly valid reason for her to be in there, and there's probably nothing special about her other than those gorgeous glossy eyes that I find myself longing to see once more. I could go down there and act like I'm on my nightly patrol, but the idea of actually having to *talk* to her upon running into her is even more daunting than the prospect of talking to regular people—assuming, of course, she's *not* regular. I really don't have any significant basis for that kind of presumption, other than a funny feeling in my stomach. Or perhaps that feeling is a little south of the stomach, but it's probably best not to entertain such a notion about a living woman.

I guess I've already made up my mind about what I'm going to do, social anxiety or not, so instead of further mulling over a decision I'd made as soon as she hit that elevator button, I leave my office and head for the morgue.

"Why are you naked."

That's the only question I'm able to force past my lips, despite the existence of other, more obvious, inquiries. Like, "Why are you eating that dead baby," or "What the fuck is going on here," or "Don't you at least want some sauce to dip that in, or something."

If she were dead, I don't think I'd last more than

thirty seconds before blowing a creamy load of useless sperm into the tight coldness of her cunt, a tidal wave of white soldiers surging into the certainty of death unknown, searching frantically for something that no longer exists. The mere thought of it makes my dick stiffen a little; complete arousal is rendered impossible by her beating heart and functioning lungs, contributing to a flushed liveliness in such stark contrast to the deadness of her eyes.

Though, this cannibalism thing is certainly interesting.

Her breasts are perfect; full and round, but not too large, with nipple placement that's about as symmetrical as a guy could hope for. Her stomach is flat and toned, complemented by a butterfly navel piercing that clashes with the stern and professional demeanor I'd observed on the security feed, and it also brings to mind a potent memory that makes me feel kind of . . . I don't know, nostalgic, I guess.

There's a tattoo on her hip of a flustered-looking rabbit holding a pocket watch in one hand, and a teacup in the other. My eyes crawl over her shapely legs, folded beneath her Indian-style, and I imagine them stiff with rigor. My cock twitches at the thought.

She's sitting on a white linen bed sheet, now smeared with bits of gore, her hands and mouth stained an ugly blackish-red. Drops of blood run down her chest, between her breasts. She holds the baby as one would hold an overly large hamburger. Its stomach is gnawed open, and its face has been chewed off.

"Why are you naked," I ask again, looking at her neatly-folded clothes on the floor, a few yards away. I can see the terror in her face, even small sparks of genuine fright in her eyes; she knows I could destroy her with this, that she's been caught doing whatever the fuck this is. She'll lose her job and her license, naturally, probably do some jail time, and forever be shunned by those around her.

She opens her mouth, presumably to speak, but is only able to emit an unpleasant moaning noise, akin to a low-quality recording of a braying mule with the volume turned down. Her lips tremble. Her teeth are red.

I look her over once again, taking in her nakedness and the half-devoured infant in her hands. "I'm not going to tell anyone," I tell her. I try to make my voice sound reassuring, but my tone comes out as dull and lifeless as ever. "You don't have anything to worry about. In that respect."

Regarding me with doleful, unblinking eyes, she licks her lips and runs her tongue over her meat-speckled teeth. There's something sexy about it. I imagine striking her over the head with my flashlight, hard enough to induce instant death, and then engaging in a passionate kiss with her corpse, my own tongue lapping up the bits of flesh remaining in her mouth. Cannibalism really isn't my thing, but there's nothing wrong with getting a little kinky now and again.

"This . . . this isn't what it looks like," Helen says, her eyes flicking from me to the dead baby.

"I don't know what else it could be," I say, and then repeat, "I'm not going to tell anyone."

There's a long pause. Our eyes are locked, but hers are so devoid of life that I have to wonder if she's even seeing me.

"I'm a messy eater," she says, finally breaking eye contact and looking at the floor, like an ashamed child admitting she's wet the bed. "That's why I'm naked. I don't want to get it on my clothes."

I nod slowly. "That makes sense," I reply. "Is this a . . . regular thing for you."

There's another uncomfortable silence before she says, "Not like this. Usually I . . . Jesus, I can't be telling you this. I can't believe this is happening. I can't believe I've finally been caught." She speaks softly, slowly, with a kind of unnaturally syncopated rhythm.

I don't say anything, just stand there with blank expectance, waiting for her to continue.

She shudders, though I suspect it's not from the cold. Sighing, she says, "This is the first time I've done it *here*. At the hospital, I mean. Usually, I break into abortion clinics at night. But this one . . . it's the one from last night. The parents had no close relatives to arrange a burial, so it was just going to be incinerated."

"What happens when they notice it's missing."

"There are three guys who work down here during the day, but they each have different shifts," she explains. "They'll all assume one of the others took care of it." There's a little less fear in her voice now, and her speech flows more freely; she's confident in her method here. I am impressed.

"Is it always babies."

"Yes," she says gravely. "*Only* babies."

"Why."

"That's how it's always been. It's all I want. It's what I crave."

There's something beautiful about those three sentences. Maybe it's the way she says it—dreamy and distant, like she's not speaking to me but to herself, lost in a moment of introspection. It's as if she's searching her own words for meaning or justification. From what I can see, though, based on my assessment of this strangely selective form of cannibalism, I don't think there's any need for justification. The meaning of it is irrelevant, in the same way the meaning of my aberrant fetish is irrelevant. We are who we are, just as anyone else is. How we got that way isn't anyone's business, least of all our own.

She sets the half-eaten baby on the sheet and looks up at me. The emptiness in her eyes is tantalizing. "You're awfully calm," she says. "Your reaction to a naked woman eating a baby isn't exactly—"

"Normal."

"Yeah. Normal. Why aren't you . . . freaking out?"

I shrug. I'm starting to feel uncomfortable with the length of this conversation. This is why I avoid talking to people. Lighting a cigarette, I say, "I guess I'm not normal."

"What are you, then?"

I let a rush of smoke out of my nostrils and stare at her though the gray haze. "Misplaced," I say.

"But aren't you—"

"You should get dressed," I say. "Clean all this up. I have to . . . check the monitors."

I don't really have to check the monitors.

I can see her muscles tense up and her brow crease with fear. Her eyes remain the same. "Wait . . . just . . . do you swear you—"

"I have to check the monitors," I say again. When tears well up in her blank eyes, I say, "Listen, I swear. It's fine."

"But I—"

"Clean all this up. I have to go check the monitors."

She's all I can think about on the drive home. Lying in bed, she's still all I can think about.

Cannibalism.

Dead babies.

Nakedness.

How long has she been at the hospital? How long has this been going on? Why am I so fascinated by her? The deadness in her eyes, perhaps, or her bizarre idea of fun, maybe. Probably both. *Definitely* both. Shit, I'm not the only psycho at Preston Druse. Maybe there are more. Maybe everyone there is some sort of freak and I'm, gawd forbid, another commonplace cog in a system of which I never wanted any part. Maybe the system is a little different than I thought, and I really am nobody extraordinary.

Nah.

I think, with mounting certainty, that I have merely stumbled across another individual whose hobbies exist outside of societal norms. We're the organic entities operating independently of the machine. The machine is the enemy. The machine is death. And not the good kind, either.

All those gears and moving parts would just tear up my dick. No thanks, I want no part of it. I will *be* no part of it.

And, apparently, neither will Helen Winchester.

I want to know more about her.

For the first time in my life, a living being has piqued my interest.

I'm already getting up to open the security office door before Helen even knocks. I've been watching her again, studying her, trying to figure out how she could be so alluringly similar to me, whilst being so disappointingly different, so I knew when she was coming my way.

As soon as the door is open, without bothering with a superfluous greeting, she asks, "Are you busy?"

I raise my eyebrows. I don't even know what that word means. "Swamped," I say, though sarcasm has never been a strong suit of mine, so I'm not sure if she's going to catch it.

She does, apparently, because she brushes past me and collapses into the extra chair propped against the wall. I sit back down in my own seat and look at her, waiting for her to speak.

"I'm extremely distressed," she says, not meeting my gaze. "Before you . . . *caught* me, I was able to, more or less, suppress the disgust I have for myself, but now it's all bubbling up to the surface."

This is all very disarming. Last night, I was just the guy who caught her naked in the morgue, eating a baby, and now it appears I'm someone she can talk to about the disgust she feels for herself. Maybe I struck her as a good listener.

"I'm . . . sorry," I say, thinking such a response

would be the most human way to approach the conversation.

"I had a dream last night," she goes on, ignoring my halfhearted apology, probably because she recognizes it as exactly that. "About a toilet baby."

I blink. "A toilet baby," I repeat. Now we're talking about toilet babies. She hasn't even bothered to formally introduce herself.

"I walked into a stall on the second-floor restroom, and there it was," she says, still not making eye contact. "There was some blood on the toilet seat, and a few drops on the floor, but the water was clear. The umbilical cord was wrapped around its neck, and its face was blue. Then, I got on my knees and I scooped it out of the toilet, and I started eating it. I didn't hesitate. I *devoured* it. But then it started to taste funny—"

Started to taste funny.

"—and I looked down at my hands, and they were covered in shit. Then I spat, and this big wet glob of shit came out, so I ran to the mirror, and my whole face was covered in it . . . huge streaks of dark brown shit all over my lips and cheeks and running down my neck. I woke up screaming. I could taste it in my mouth—the shit, I mean. I puked all over my bed."

I nod slowly, but I can't think of anything to say.

"So?" she says, finally raising her eyes to lock with mine. "What do you think it means?"

"I'm a security guard," I tell her. "I don't specialize in dream interpretation." After a brief but purposeful pause, I say, "Listen, um . . . Dr. Winchester, I don't even know you."

She takes a deep breath and sighs through her

teeth. "Right," she says, "I'm sorry. I'm just . . . I don't know." She drums her lacquer-nailed fingers on her thigh and then takes a brown pill bottle from her pocket, shaking five big white tablets onto her palm. I hand her my Diet Coke, and she tosses her head back and swallows them.

"What are those," I ask.

She looks at me for a moment, and I can tell she's considering whether or not she should lie. "Vicodin," she says. "I get chronic migraines." Then, almost as an afterthought, "They're prescribed to me."

I believe they're Vicodin, and she probably *does* get migraines, but the bottle had been plain and unmarked, without the traditional white label sticker. Furthermore, I don't know much about drugs, but I don't think any self-respecting doctor would prescribe five opiate pills of that size for a headache.

It suddenly makes sense, though—her eyes. She's *stoned*. Her eyes look glassy and dead because she's getting high on pain medication.

Substance abuse has never been my thing. Alcohol makes me dizzy and sick. The first, and only, time I got drunk resulted in a hangover so obscene that I have since stayed true to that morning's solemnly-sworn Porcelain Pledge. I smoked pot once in high school, with a foreign exchange student from Uganda (whose English vocabulary was humorously limited to phrases he picked up on while binging on American internet porn), but it just made me feel nervous and jittery. It didn't help that, every time he passed the joint to me, he would say things like, "Come on my titties", or "Lick my asshole, you fuck". I don't think he knew what he was saying, but it nevertheless made an already uncomfortable experience even more awkward. Since then, I've seen no reason to give drugs another go.

That being said, I find myself unbothered by Helen's apparent addiction to pharmaceuticals. For one, it's certainly more respectable than guzzling Bud Light out of a beer bong, or smoking joints on her lunch break—the latter being something I'm certain the day guard does quite frequently, judging from the security footage I found of him locking himself in storage rooms, and the lingering skunky smells I've noticed within them. I could report him, but that would require more fucks than I have to give.

"I'm not a junkie, or anything like that," Helen says, nervously fidgeting at her fingernails.

"I know," I say. Of course, I *don't* know, but what does anyone really know, anyway.

"I don't want you to think I'm some sort of drug addict."

"Why do you care what I think."

She shrugs and looks down at her worrying hands. "I guess I just . . . you *saw* me. You saw me doing what I do, and you weren't even fazed. You could have turned me in, but you didn't. I think just about anyone else would have."

"I'm not seeing your point."

"I want to know *why*. I want to know what you want with me. Are you planning on blackmailing me?"

"No."

She sighs again, a sound that, from her, is strangely erotic despite the fact that any form of respiration should be a complete turnoff to me. "Then what do you *want?*" she asks, her voice exasperated and pleading.

"I don't want anything. I just don't think there's anything wrong with what you do."

She takes off her glasses and folds them neatly in her lap, blinking her dead eyes at me with her head cocked and her lips pursed. "I eat dead babies," she says. "What do you mean you don't see anything *wrong* with it? If that's true, you must have a really fucked-up sense of right and wrong."

"Hey," I say, "I have sex with dead girls."

I immediately regret saying it, but after a few moments of silence passes between us, it begins to feel almost cathartic. I have now bound myself to this woman, the same way my knowledge of her secret binds her to me, and there's something thrilling about the reckless danger of it all.

She bites her lip, looking like she's trying to figure out if I'm fucking with her or not. "Dead girls?" she asks. "You . . . have *sex* with them? As in, corpses?"

She sounds intrigued instead of appalled, so I continue and say, "Yes, I fuck corpses. In the morgue. At least three or four times a month. Sometimes more."

She blinks at me as her lips quiver into a small, dopey smile. "That's . . . remarkable."

I raise my eyebrows again. "I. Have. Sex. With. Dead girls." I glance awkwardly at the security monitors as if there would actually be anything of note on them, and even if there was, I'm too distracted to be able to notice it. "What do you mean, 'remarkable.'"

Her smile widens. "I mean, it's even stranger than what I do."

I blink at her, take off my glasses, and rub my eyes. "I wouldn't go that far," I say evenly. "You eat babies."

The smile vanishes from her face and her cheeks flush. "Yes, well, right. I wasn't being judgmental. It's ironic, is all. This whole thing. It's all very . . . ironic."

"That's a cute word for it."

"Do you have a better one?"

"'Coincidental', maybe. That's not really what 'irony' means. Plus, I think that Alanis Morissette song would have been a lot less popular if it had had references to cannibalism and necrophilia."

The corners of her mouth twitch into an almost-smirk. "You don't strike me as the kind of person who listens to Alanis Morissette," she says.

"I'm not."

She tilts her head to the side a little and studies me. "What kind of person *are* you, then?"

"I'm not any kind of person." I consider this for a moment before amending, "I'm the kind of person who has sex with dead girls."

"I'd imagine that probably falls somewhere on the scale between 'tortured emo artist' and 'heavy metal burnout'," she says. Her eyes twinkle a little, which repulses me; I wish they'd stay dead-looking. She should take some more pills. "You probably listen to music like Hawthorne Heights and, I don't know, As I Lay Dying, right?"

"No," I say with a grimace, and then, "Don't try to psychoanalyze me."

"I'm sorry, I didn't mean—"

"Listen, you should go. I'm sorry you had a bad dream, and I'm sorry I can't help you interpret it. Google it, or something."

She looks flustered by my brusqueness, but stands up and primly smooths out the creases in the front of her white coat. "All right," she says with a curt nod, "I'm sorry to have disturbed you." She starts to leave but stops and gestures to the book lying open on my desk, a weathered paperback copy of *The Pleasures of the Damned.* "If you like Bukowski, read some Will Self. Start with *My Idea of Fun.*"

An unexpected plot twist—she *reads*, and apparently with good taste. She must notice something from my reaction, because she smiles. "If you like that one," she says, "I'll tell you where to go from there. You know where to find me."

And then she's gone, with a fluid rapidity that calls into question whether she'd been there at all. Blink once, blink twice. Her absence carries more weight than did her presence. If this were a movie, I'd go after her. Real life isn't as dramatic.

Color me boring.

And no, I really *don't* listen to Hawthorne Heights.

I can't seem to get rid of her, nor can I seem to find myself appropriately troubled by this.

She comes to my office every night. Sometimes, when she's really high, she just sits there with her head lolling, watching me read. At first, it made me nervous. Now, I am unbothered, and I don't know why.

Usually, though, she's coherent enough to talk to me, and I just listen, for the most part. She keeps telling me about her fucked-up dreams, about her constant car problems, about the lazy and incompetent nurses. Sometimes, I offer halfhearted input. I tell her to fire the nurses. I tell her to get a new car. She always shrugs and keeps on talking.

A couple of weeks pass, and she keeps visiting me and telling me things I don't want to hear, but don't really mind hearing, either. I *do*, admittedly, somewhat enjoy the stories of her escapades into abortion clinics, and the way she describes the taste of dead infant flesh. It's soft and moist, she says, and incredibly tender, like slightly undercooked veal sweetened with a dusting of brown sugar. She says it has a way of melting in your mouth. Some parts of it are jelly-like. The fat is soft but tough, and she savors the time it takes to grind it down.

Each baby is a little different, she says, but they all share the same traits, in regard to the general taste.

She tells me they're all delicious, every one of them, down to the last bite.

I ask her if she ever adds anything for additional flavor.

She says she doesn't have to.

She says that would ruin it.

"I don't know if this is related," she says, "but I had a baby brother when I was a child, named Jason. I was six years old when he died. I was the one who found him. I still dream about it. I think it . . . really fucked me up." She looks at her hands and fidgets with them. I wait for her to continue, but she doesn't.

"How did he die," I ask her.

She doesn't answer at first. When she does, her voice is very low and I have to strain to hear her. "I had this ferret," she murmurs. "His name was Samson. I loved that ferret. My parents got him for me when he was only a few weeks old, and he was my best friend. He wasn't like most ferrets, where they just run around and do their own thing and ignore everyone, for the most part. He was like a dog. He was always at my heels, and he slept with me every night. I would snuggle him close and go to sleep to the sound of his breath."

She stops, and I want to ask her how a ferret is related to her dead brother, but then it occurs to me, and I know the ending of the story already.

"One night, I woke up and he wasn't there," she continues. I realize I'm kind of excited to hear the rest. I told you how much I hate babies, and the thought of Helen's ferret smothering an infant in its crib is pretty great. "I got up, and I looked all over for him, but I couldn't find him. Then I went into Jason's room."

Aw, shit, it's about to get so good.

"And there he was," Helen says. "There he was." She pops a few pills and I hand her my Diet Coke, and then she says, "In the crib. Samson was in the crib. He had smothered Jason."

Right on, Samson, right on.

"There's more, though," Helen says. "After he had smothered him, he had . . . he . . . he'd started eating him. He'd started eating Jason's face."

Yikes, didn't see that part coming.

"There wasn't much left by the time I found him. Of Jason's face, I mean. All the flesh had been eaten away, and you could see his skull. I screamed and my parents came running in, and then *they* screamed. My mom threw up and then fainted in her own puke. My dad ran over and picked Samson up, he threw him so hard against the wall that his head broke open and some of his brains started to come out."

She's crying now. I'm supposed to comfort her—I think any decent human being would—but I'm not a decent human being, and I don't know much about comfort, so I just sit and wait for her to finish telling the story.

"My dad picked up little Jason and held him and cried and cried, and screamed at God to bring him back. And do you know what *I* did?"

I shake my head.

"I ran over to Samson and held him and sobbed into his fur. His blood got on my pajamas, and I screamed when I realized how much blood there was. I didn't care about Jason. Or my mother, who ended up drowning in the puddle of her vomit while my dad and I screamed and cried, him over my brother and me over my ferret." She pauses to wipe her eyes, and I get some tissues out of one of the desk drawers and hand them to her. She blows her nose, bunches up the tissue in her fists in a manner that's almost hateful, and then says, "Samson didn't know what he was doing. He didn't deserve to die."

"No," I say, nodding my head in genuine agreement. "No, he didn't."

"Nothing was really the same after that," Helen says.

"Yeah," I say. "That makes sense."

The two of us are quiet for a very long time. She cries a little more and I keep thinking about the ferret eating the baby, and I have to fold my hands over my crotch to conceal my half-hardon.

I'm about to ask if she wants to smoke, when she suddenly starts up again with another story. "I was thirteen when I had my first one," she tells me. "I was walking in the woods, and I found this little bundle wrapped up in a basket. Someone had just left it there. It hadn't been dead long." She looks at me, as if expecting me to tell her to stop. When I don't, she goes on, her voice still hushed, "I don't know why my first thought was to eat it. To take a big bite out of it and see how it tasted. Maybe it was the smell. It just smelled so good. So, I did. I started with its face. I took a bite, and then I took another, and before I knew it, I'd pretty much gnawed it down to the bone. I ate so much I threw up, but even the vomit tasted delicious."

I realize I'm leaning forward, enraptured.

She shakes out a couple more pills, and I give her my Coke. She washes them down and then says, "I couldn't stop thinking about it. For the longest time, it was *all* I thought about. I stopped thinking about Samson and Jason, and I started thinking about babies. More time passed, and I was able to deal with the cravings, but I never forgot."

"When was the next time," I ask.

"Med school," she answers. "I'd waited so long. We dissected them for class, and then afterward, late at night, I sneaked in and stole one and took it home with me. I *feasted* upon it, and . . . " She trails off, frowning, looking away. "And it was then that I knew there was something seriously wrong with me."

I raise my eyebrows. "You didn't think there was something wrong with you after the first one," I ask, bemused.

She shrugs. "I was young. Sure, I knew it was a bit strange, but I guess I never acknowledged the correlation between what I'd done, and what that said about me as a human being. I craved it, but I suppressed the notion of what it really was. And that . . . that just makes me more fucked up. It wasn't until the *second* act of cannibalism that I realized what I was."

"What are you," I ask her.

"A monster."

I lean back in my chair and tell her, "That seems a little extreme."

"People aren't supposed to eat babies."

I swivel casually in my chair, twiddling my thumbs. "People aren't supposed to do a lot of the things that they do. People aren't supposed to fuck dead girls, but that doesn't make me a monster. It just makes me different. It makes me . . . separate. From everything. From everyone. I am enlightened."

I notice there are tears in her eyes. She wipes them away with her long-fingered white hands and says, "It would be nice if I could look at it like you do."

I stare hard into her bleary eyes and say, "Who says you can't."

"Everything I know to be true."

"Nothing you know to be true, is true. Society has brainwashed you. Don't be like the rest. Fuck the rest."

She nods, unconvinced. "I have to go," she says. "I think I'm supposed to deliver a baby tonight, or something. I don't know. I can't keep my schedule straight anymore."

"Okay," I say.

She leaves. I'd pity her if I was capable of it.

Helen and I sit outside under the entryway awning, passing a cigarette back and forth, staring at the fat fullness of the moon, and listening to the moths mindlessly slapping against the light above the main door. She is close, her shoulder touching mine. I can smell her modestly-applied perfume, and the lingering scent of shampoo in her hair. Her proximity should feel smothering, I should be crawling in my skin, but for once, the physical closeness of another living being is entirely tolerable. Almost, dare I say, *pleasant*. Not quite, but almost.

"How did it start?" she asks. I can feel her looking at me, though I don't return her gaze. "As in, when did you realize you were like this, and what did you do about it? I told you my story. It's your turn, now."

The question takes me by surprise, and there's really no easy or definitive answer. I've always known I was different, that I thought differently from other people, saw things in a different light, a *darker* light, but for a long time I didn't know there was anything I could do about it. I had no urges, no aberrant lust— I was just *different*, painfully so. I was perpetually uncomfortable, unbearably insecure, and in my angst-ridden tween years I even became borderline suicidal, always one wrong word away from slashing my wrists or swallowing Drano. I felt like a disfigured monster whenever I was around other people, convinced they saw me for the alien I was, and that they hated me for it. My mom sent me to therapy, but that only made me feel even worse.

It wasn't until my fifteenth year that things started to come together and make a semblance of sense. By then I had, for some time, begun to really experience the sexually-frustrated horror that is puberty. My body had desires that conflicted clashingly with my conscious mind. A short skirt or low-cut top would set off maddening twinges of "lust", for want of a better word, but the thought of actually being *naked* in front of a woman made me sick with terror. How could anyone want to strip bare before another human being, opening himself up to the very real possibility of endless judgment, spoken or otherwise? And even if you were somehow able to endure the inevitability of her silently scrutinizing eyes, and provided she didn't cast you out in disgust, you then had to actually get *close* to her, *touch* her, and worse, let *her* touch *you*. The thought was unthinkable.

From about the time I was twelve, until I was fifteen, my loins were at constant war with my brain, the latter doing everything in its power to suppress my confused libido. I had no outlet; even masturbation was a nauseating impossibility, resulting in a steady stream of contorted nightmares from which I would awaken to semen-soaked underwear, due to my body's need to relieve the pressure in my groin since I wasn't doing it myself. I started washing my own sheets. My mother didn't ask questions. By then, she had learned not to ask questions.

And then, like a glorious gift from the gods themselves, there came the night of *the party*.

I really had no business being invited—I had no friends and I avoided conversation by any means necessary, blatant rudeness notwithstanding—but the guy who was hosting it had been absently handing out invitations to everyone in the hall after the final bell rang, as all the students were stampeding for the exit, and one of the unsealed envelopes somehow ended up in my hand amidst the confusion.

To this day, I'm still not sure what compelled me to actually go. My mother was spending the weekend in Hong Kong or Moscow or something, for some sort of business conference, and as I sat reading in the dim light of my room that Saturday night, I found myself unable to concentrate on the words, my mind wandering to curious musings about what a high school party might actually be like. The invitation taunted me from my nightstand. The address printed on it was less than a block from my house. I could go check it out, and if it was as awful as I suspected, I could be back at home without having sacrificed any sizable amount of my night.

So, yes, I went, and yes, it was awful. One of the football players took my coat at the door and told me it would be upstairs in the first room on the left. Another one, already sloppy drunk, clapped me on the back and handed me a beer and slurred something about communists in the school administration. I sipped the beer, hating the taste of it more and more with each swallow, and wandered from room to room, not talking to anyone but trying desperately not to appear as awkward as I felt. The music was loud and annoying, and the snippets of overheard conversation were boring. I don't think anyone really noticed me, which was for the best. When the beer was half gone and I was sure one more sip would make me puke, I threw it out and went upstairs to claim my coat.

The room was dark, but I could make out the pile of coats piled haphazardly in the corner. When I turned on the light, though, my eye was caught by something else.

A girl.

On the bed.

Unconscious.

I recognized her. She was a senior, and a cheerleader or a volleyball player, too, I think. Very popular, very pretty. Long blonde hair and tan, muscular legs that went on for miles. She was wearing short jean cutoffs, despite the cold late-October weather, and a loose-fitting sweater that hung off one shoulder. It had ridden up her stomach when she'd fallen onto the bed, exposing a flat, golden-bronze midriff, and a butterfly navel piercing.

I approached her, not breathing.

Poking her leg very softly, I whispered, "Um, hey, are you okay." Of course, I didn't care if she was okay—I just wanted to make sure she wasn't going to wake up. My mind had already decided everything for me, but I had to be sure she was going to remain drunkenly comatose. Judging by the empty bottle of Grey Goose on the floor, and the slow, heavy raggedness of her breathing, I thought my chances of that looked pretty good.

I poked her again, then shook her, and finally slapped her across the face. Nothing.

I closed the bedroom door and locked it.

My entire body was shaking as I undressed her. First, the shoes and shorts, sucking her toes, running my hands over her smooth thighs. I then peeled her shirt over her head and tossed it aside, hungrily seizing the great globes of her breasts and squeezing them as hard as I dared. I think my eyes probably rolled back in my head. I don't remember. I didn't remove the bra because I was afraid I wouldn't be able to redo the clasp when it came time to put her clothes back on, but I did peel the cups down so I could peek at her huge round nipples, kissing them and flicking them.

My heart was racing so fast I feared it might charge up my throat and burst out of my mouth, only to die pitifully on the bed next to her. There was also the ever-present notion that she could wake up at any time to find herself being molested by a creepy little freshman, in a locked bedroom that was not her own.

When neither of these things happened, I slowly pulled off her white silk panties, pausing for a brief observation of her pubic region before stepping out of my jeans and underwear.

"I'm going to fuck you, now," I whispered weakly. "I promise I'll be quick. Don't be mad if you wake up."

I had to clamp a hand over my mouth to keep from crying out when I first slid into her; there was some resistance at first, but it was followed by a tight, suction-like feeling for which I had not been prepared, and it was incredible. I do remember thinking, however, that it wasn't *quite* right. There was that nagging terror that she'd wake up, and her proximity was unnerving, unconscious or not. Still, my body hungered for this, and with four quick pumps I was done, collapsing onto her and gasping into her neck.

I didn't dare lie there for long, so I got up and hastily dressed her, and then myself, before grabbing my coat and walking back downstairs as casually as I could, sneaking out the back door and running home.

"Hello? Are you still with me?" Helen is looking at me expectantly, glassy eyes piercing my own.

"Sorry," I say. "I . . . spaced out."

"So . . . how did it start?" she asks again.

I shrug. "I guess some people are just born fucked up."

She blinks slowly, and I can tell she knows I'm not telling her something, but she doesn't press the issue.

"I don't think you're fucked up," she says. "I'm the one who's fucked up. I think what you do is . . . kind of beautiful, actually. Beautiful and pure. You recognize your own unique tastes, and you act upon them unabashedly."

"I mean, so do you."

She shakes her head and gently takes the cigarette from me, dragging thoughtfully and then flicking it out onto the asphalt as she exhales. "No, with me it's different. I'm *afraid*. All the time. Can you imagine the things they'd say about me in the papers? The way people would look at me? They'd lock me away and scorn me for the leper I am. They'd call me 'the Maternity Monster', or something. A doctor trusted to bring new life from the womb of womankind, who secretly devours dead fetuses. The damnation would be unending, and the fear of it haunts my every waking moment, and most of my dreams, as well. *You*, though, you're so calm and unafraid. You just do what you do, and you don't seem to have a shred of anxiety of what will happen if you're found out."

I don't entertain the notion of getting caught, because I don't see it as a possibility. Not yet, anyway.

I'm confident enough in my own discretion to believe my sex life will remain uninterrupted until I'm able to carry out my future plans. My foundation is solid.

Speaking of babies, though, I should mention that the girl from the party ended up getting pregnant. She naturally assumed it had been her boyfriend, a dauntingly tall fellow on the varsity basketball team who stayed out of trouble and was a favorite for the valedictorian title that year. Who knows. Maybe it *was* his, but the timing seemed a little too coincidental for that.

Whatever the case, the girl decided to abort the pregnancy, a choice she claimed to have been her own, despite rumors that it had been the squeaky-clean boyfriend who had talked her into it. A few weeks after the procedure, she slashed her wrists in the bathtub, purportedly while listening to Enya. I spent a solid fifteen seconds somewhat distraught over my disturbing lack of guilt.

I didn't go to the funeral, either, but I did break into the funeral home for another go at her. She was infinitely better the second time.

Because there was no chance of her waking up.

Because she was dead.

I had found my true calling.

It also stands to be said that fucking a corpse in a coffin provides for a morbid eroticism that is absolutely to die for. Yes, that pun was wholly intended, and yes, I *do* find myself amusing. The audience doesn't get it, but that's what laugh tracks are for.

Thus began a four-year-long habit of sneaking into funeral homes and having my way with the newly dead, lasting until I landed the job here at the hospital; it's a lot easier—and safer—to engage in my behavior when the corpses are just a keycard-swipe away.

"We're not hurting anyone," I say, making an effort to refocus my attention on Helen. I light another cigarette. "The girls I fuck, the babies you eat—they're already dead."

She brushes a lock of hair from her face and looks out at the parking lot. I hand her the cigarette, and she takes it. "It's the principle of it," she says. "What I do is . . . it's sick. You don't know how terribly I wish I could be like other people. While everyone else is getting all gaga over a newborn, all I can think about is how good it would taste. Other people have favorite foods, like pizza or apple pie or something, and mine is fucking *aborted fetuses*, for Christ's sake."

I shrug. "Other people watch porn, but I jack off to *Night of the Living Dead*."

She looks at me blankly for a few seconds, blinking her big dead-ish eyes, and then bursts into laughter. "Thank you," she says in between giggles. "I needed that."

I hadn't been trying to be funny, but hey, whatever works.

"Seriously, though," she goes on once she's gotten ahold of herself. "I would *kill* for normalcy. To be able to live life like a regular human being, instead of suffering this constant, plaguing hunger of dead infant flesh."

I'm suddenly annoyed. "*Normalcy?*" I ask, louder than is probably necessary, surprising myself with the unusual amount of animated expression in my voice.

"*A regular human being*? Jesus, what the fuck is there in *that*? What does that even *mean*? Credit card debt, a mortgage, a nagging spouse and bratty kids and a minivan and a fucking family pet? A nine-to-five job that you hate, and that'll kill you before you ever see your fabled 401k? Cocktail parties and parent-teacher conferences and suburban cul-de-sacs? Monogamous sex, and the obligatory midlife crisis? Potpourri? Wall fixtures? Christmas cards? A welcome mat and a mailbox with your name stenciled on it in fancy lettering? Shitty diapers and foreign nannies and *Goodnight Moon?* Cramming your face with potato chips while watching primetime television? Antidepressants and crash diets, Coach purses and Italian sunglasses? Boxed wine and light beer and mentholated cigarettes? Pediatrician visits and orthodontist bills and college funds? Book clubs, PTA meetings, labor unions, special interest groups, yoga class, the fucking neighborhood *watch*? Dinner table gossip and conspiracy theories? How about old age, menopause, saggy tits, and rocking chairs on the porch? Or better yet, leukemia, dementia, emphysema, adult Depends, feeding tubes, oxygen tanks, false teeth, cirrhosis, kidney failure, heart disease, osteoporosis, and dying days spent having your ass wiped by STNAs in a stuffy nursing home reeking of death and disinfectant? Is *that* the kind of normalcy you lust for so much? All of that—is *that* worth the title of *regular human being*? Is it, Helen? *Is it?*"

I'm out of breath, my chest heaving, my jaw aching from its strenuous spurt of exercise, to which it is quite unaccustomed. I wipe sweat from my brow with the back of my hand and spark up yet another smoke. The one in Helen's hand has gone out.

Her glossy eyes are wide, her mouth slightly agape. My hands are shaking, and my cigarette slips from between my fingers, onto the pavement. I stare at it for a few moments before picking it back up and tremblingly placing it in my mouth.

"My God," Helen says, eyes still bewildered and saucer-shaped, magnified all the more by the thick lenses of her glasses. "You know, you haven't spoken more than a few short sentences at a time since I met you. That was unusually . . . eloquent. You're so mellow and monotone, all the time. You're never expressive about anything."

Shrugging, I say, "Sometimes I can be. Around the dead. When I'm talking to dead girls, I'm . . . different. You struck a sensitive chord in me, I guess. I hate normalcy. My parents were normal. I hated my parents."

"Where are they now?"

"Dead. My father died in a car accident when I was eight, and my mother had a heart attack at a budget meeting in Tokyo just before I turned eighteen."

"That's awful."

"No, it's not. They were burdensome. And they left me a lot of money." I finish my cigarette and then polish the lenses of my glasses with my sleeve.

"I envy the ease with which you can dismiss things."

"Envy is wasteful and purposeless."

She smiles, and it is a cold smile, made colder still by the icy, pale-blue lifelessness in her stoned eyes. "Isn't everything?"

This gives me brief pause, and I'm impressed by the shrewdness of her response. It reminds me of why I can tolerate her, why I might even, dare I say it, *like* her. "Yes," I say, "I guess it is."

The death smell isn't particularly strong, but it's there, and it leads me to a room occupied by a sleeping girl. It's hard to say how old she is, because her face is so fucked up. Both eyes have been beaten to blue-tinged black, her nose is a trifle askew, and her cheeks, forehead, and mouth are decorated with small-to-medium-sized cuts. There's dried blood in her dishwater-blonde hair. She is beautiful.

I sit in the chair next to her and look at the chart hanging from her bed. Tamara R. Jericho, twenty-one years old, of Villa Vida, OH. As I'm skimming through the description of her injuries—rape by at least four separate assailants, multiple stab wounds in the torso and abdominal areas, vaginal lesions, broken nose, second-degree burns on thighs; the list goes on—she awakens and looks at me. She blinks sleep out of her eyes, squints at me, and asks, "Are you another doctor?"

I think about bolting from the room to avoid conversation, but she's heavily sedated, so I relax a little and tell her no, I'm not a doctor.

She smiles a little and lets out a small sigh that I guess signifies relief. "Good," she says. "I'm so sick of doctors. I don't know why they won't just leave me alone and let me die."

I try to think of something to say and can't, so we

sit there in awkward silence for a few moments before I finally blurt out, "Sorry you got raped."

She giggles, which surprises me. I may not be an expert on human emotion, but I know that laughter isn't the appropriate response to my statement. Women don't like to be raped. Not while they're alive, at least.

"Don't be sorry," she says, reaching out and putting her hand over mine. "It was wonderful."

I simply look at her with my head to the side and say, "Um . . . what."

"There's just something about being raped. I love it."

I definitely don't know what to say in response to that.

"There were four of them," she goes on. "They took turns with me for hours. They beat me and stabbed me and burned me."

"Yeah. I read your chart."

"I was completely powerless. They bound me with ropes and zip ties. I mean, I couldn't have moved anyway, I was so beat up. They had total control. And for me, it's all . . . about . . . *control*."

"What is," I ask.

"*Everything*. I like to just let go. But with sex . . . that's when powerlessness feels the best. And . . . I *love* sex." She sighs, and it looks like the action pains her.

"Why are you telling me all of this."

She smiles again, and this seems to pain her, too. One of the cuts on her cheek starts to bleed. "I'm going to die," she says, "and you're the only one there is to tell. Besides, you're fucked up, too. Not fucked up in the way that *I* am, but there's something wrong with you. I can tell. I can see it in you."

My heartbeat quickens. "What do you see," I ask her. My voice is trembling and uneasy, and I wonder if she notices it. I suspect she does.

No, I *know* she does.

"I'm not sure, exactly. It's more what I *can't* see, I guess. Something's missing inside of you. Something that should be there . . . but isn't."

I look down at the sparkling white tile, running a hand through my hair. "Life," I say. "That's what you're not seeing. I don't have any life inside of me."

Her smile widens, making two more cuts begin to bleed. "Yes," she says. "That's exactly what it is."

"I'm going to fuck you, you know. Once you're dead. I'm going to fuck your corpse after you die."

She's not at all taken aback by this. Instead, she says, "Good. I'm looking forward to it. I'm sure I'll enjoy it very much."

Nothing this girl says surprises me at this point. "You'll be dead," I tell her. "How could you enjoy it if you're dead."

"Oh, I *always* enjoy sex. I've enjoyed it all my life, ever since I was seven. Why shouldn't I enjoy it when I'm dead? Be rough with me, though, would you? I love rough sex. Probably because I've been raped so many times."

Not being a conversationalist, most discussions I've had with people, that lasted more than a few minutes, usually ended up getting weird. I always say something that freaks the other person out. Typically, it's by accident.

This is how those people must feel.

I know I should probably get up and go and leave this girl to die, but I'm somehow magnetized to her, in a similar way that I'm magnetized to Helen. I suppose there's just something about meeting someone who's even more fucked up than you are.

"You've been having sex since you were seven," I ask her.

She nods, grinning, blood running down her cheeks in narrow rivulets. "It started with my uncle. I know that's a cliché, but that's just the way it was. He'd give me brandy and get me drunk, then he'd rape the shit out of me. I loved every minute of it, right from the very first time. It went on for years, and once I got a little older, I started fucking him in this consensual sort of way, and I guess we kind of became lovers, but it wasn't as good. It's always better when it's forceful, violent . . . *out of my control.*"

I notice her face is paler than it had been when I'd first come in. I can see goosebumps on her flesh. She's shivering and she retracts her arm, burying it under the blanket. The death smell is getting stronger, radiating off her. She doesn't have long.

"It's close," she says. "I know. Don't feel bad for me. This is the way I've always wanted to die. I'm very lucky. How many people get to die exactly the way they want to?"

"Not many people want to be stabbed and gang raped to death," I say. "Not many people want to die at all. I think they try not to think about it."

"I'm not afraid. I've always thought about death a lot."

"I have, too."

"I know."

My mouth twitches, and I drum my fingers on my thighs. I don't want to sit here and watch her die. I stand and say, "I have to go. I have to check the monitors."

She nods and says, "I can't wait for you to fuck me. I like you. I like that you're so fucked up."

I nod, put my hands in my pockets, look around, nod again, and then leave.

I set one of the monitors to that room and watch as the doctors come in and fail to resuscitate her, then wheel her down to the morgue. I wait a whole five minutes after they leave the morgue and return upstairs before I go down and fuck her.

I can't wait until tomorrow.

I'm rough with her.

Really rough.

Rough enough that I tear the piercings from her nipples and shove them down her throat, just for the hell of it.

Rough enough that I pretend to strangle her, and then punch the soft pillows of her breasts, and dig my fingers into the gashes in her flesh from the knives of her attackers.

Rough enough that, instead of coming in her cunt, I pull out and stab my dick into a particularly large wound in her thigh, squeezing my semen into her leg.

I don't look at her face, because I'm afraid she'll be smiling up at me.

"My car wouldn't start tonight. I had to take the RTA." Helen has let herself into my office again. If it were anyone else, I'd start locking the door.

"That's tragic," I say. My lack of tone could be interpreted as sarcasm, but it's not; public transportation is one of my greatest fears. I think school buses have that effect on square peg children. Or maybe I'm just special like that.

And maybe Jesus is my fucking sunbeam.

"I live in a nice area," Helen says, "so, where all the vagrants on that bus came from, I don't know."

"Where do you live."

"Villa Vida. There's only one bus stop in the whole town, and it's a mile from my house. I would have taken a cab, but I never carry cash."

"Attractive women shouldn't be walking around by themselves in the middle of the night." I think of Tamara Jericho. Tamara Jericho from Villa Vida, who got raped to death and enjoyed it.

Her mouth smiles. Her ghost eyes don't. "You think I'm attractive. I think that's the first nice thing you've said to me."

"Let's not make a big thing out of it."

She shrugs. "I wasn't in any real danger. Villa Vida is a nice little suburban community. Nothing ever happens there."

"Things happen everywhere," I say, thinking of how tight Tamara's dead cunt had been, in spite of all the past rapes. "Villa Vida isn't special. It just thinks it is."

"Where do you live?"

"Millhaven," I say. "In a studio apartment above the Bad Seed."

She thinks for a second, then wrinkles her nose and says, "That shitty little dive bar on Jubilee Street? Why would you live *there* if you've got all that money your parents left you?"

"Money and possessions don't mean anything to me. I don't care about where I live, or what I own. I get satisfaction through one thing, and that's it. The money is nice only because it keeps me from having to worry about money."

She nods slowly. "I see. I guess that makes sense."

"Why are we talking about this. Why does it matter where I live."

"I wanted to know if you live close by. I was hoping you could maybe give me a ride home, if it's not too far out of the way. I really don't want to have to suffer through the bus thing again."

You have to pass Villa Vida going to Millhaven from here, and she knows that. If I decline, she'll know I'm just being a dick. Normally that wouldn't bother me, but for whatever reason, I am somewhat invested in her opinion of me.

Yuck.

"Okay," I say.

She smiles, and this time her eyes sort of do, too.

Yuck.

"What time do you get off?" she asks.

I make a show of looking at the cheap drugstore Timex on my wrist. "Fifteen minutes," I say.

"I really appreciate this. Can I, like, buy you breakfast or something?"

"No."

Her expression turns crestfallen at my answer. She's showing too much emotion on her face; it must have been awhile since her last painkiller dose. I wonder if it would be rude of me to suggest she take some more. Emotions gross me out, especially when they're visible.

People gross me out.

Especially when they're visible.

I suppose Helen, though, is exempt from that rule, for the time being.

She just needs to take some more pills.

She looks questioningly at my car and says, "*This* is what you drive?"

It's a beat up old black Toyota, rust on the fenders, a dent in the rear driver's side door. It's got something, like, 150,000 miles on it. It treats me well, and I've only had to take it to the shop a few times, for minor repairs.

"I get that you don't need a big fancy apartment or anything, but if you've got money, wouldn't you at least want to buy a decent car?"

"It is decent," I say, getting in and starting the ignition. Helen gives the car a subtle look of disapproval as she walks around to get in on the other side. She has to yank on the handle a couple times to get the door open. Sometimes it gets jammed.

She turns on the cassette player as I start driving. I've thought about having a CD player installed, but can never be bothered enough to do it. There's a Ministry tape playing, and she says appreciatively, "*The Mind is a Terrible Thing to Taste.* This is their best album, I think, next to *With Sympathy.*"

"*With Sympathy* sucks," I tell her, pulling out of the parking lot and onto the road. "I've never even been able to listen to the whole thing." As I get on the on ramp for the freeway, she skips the tape to track four and grins slyly at me.

"This is my favorite song on the album," she says. "As a matter of fact, it's probably my favorite song of *all* their songs."

I glance at her sideways and say, "I didn't figure you to be one for cliché."

"There's a lot of things you don't know about me," she says in a tone I think is supposed to be seductive, but I can't be sure.

"There's a lot of things I do know about you."

After a brief, uncomfortable silence, she asks, "Can we smoke in here?"

"Yeah."

"Can I have a cigarette?"

"Yeah." I hand her the pack and my lighter from my breast pocket. She lights it, exhales, and cracks the window with the manual hand crank.

The sun is starting to come up. The color of the sky makes me think of her naked in the basement, and I'm annoyed by the tingling sensation in my groin. I look over at her profile, holding the cigarette elegantly in her hand, like an English noblewoman, her hair lit a vibrant yellow by the rising sun. She catches me looking at her and I look away, hoping she doesn't notice my flushed cheeks.

"It's beautiful, isn't it?" she says, staring dreamily out the windshield and turning the music down. Al Jourgensen's shrieking voice fades to a muted murmur, emitting from the fuzzy stereo system. "The sky. It's almost like it's . . . *blushing*."

Goddammit.

"I guess," I say. "I'm not really impressed by things like that. Sunrises. Sunsets. Rainbows, eclipses, whatever."

"What *does* impress you, then?"

"You shouldn't have to ask me that, by now. I think we know each other well enough."

She sighs and looks out the side window. We're nearing Villa Vida now, entering the sordid kingdom of suburbia. She gazes out over the houses and cul-de-sacs, the churches and convenience stores, the sprawling schoolhouse compounds.

"They're all just starting to wake up," she says quietly. "All the normal people. Ready to go about their normal lives. Normal people, living normal lives, who don't eat babies."

"Or fuck dead girls," I say, and then, "So what. Fuck them. And the fancy cars they rode in on."

She looks over at me, exasperated, and says, "Do you really *never* think about what it would be like to be one of them? To have a normal life and do normal things?"

"We've already had this conversation," I say irritably. "If you want it so bad, then have it. What's stopping you. You already live in the perfect place for it."

"Babies," she says, looking down at the ash that's fallen on her thigh. She throws the cigarette out, unfinished, and then rolls the window up. "Babies are stopping me. I just . . . can't stop eating them."

You can laugh at that part. I won't judge.

We're both silent for the rest of the drive.

Once I get off at the Villa Vida exit, she directs me

to her house, which is a big, extravagant Colonial, with huge windows and thick pillars in the front. There's a shiny black Audi in the driveway. It's the kind of house you'd expect a doctor to have. I think about what I said earlier, about clichés.

I stop on the street, at the end of the driveway, and put the car in park. I look over at her. She looks back and smiles, but wanly. She looks tired. Not as stoned as usual, but tired. "Thank you," she says. "I really appreciate this."

"Yeah," I say, shifting uncomfortably in my seat. "It's . . . really not a big deal." It's hard for me to look at her when her eyes aren't as dead as I'd like them to be. The exhaustion is in her face, around her eyes, but not within them. They're still a little glassy, but I feel like she's seeing me more than she usually can, and I don't like that. I feel like a museum exhibit when people look at me, *really* look at me, instead of looking through or past me, like they usually do.

But no, right now, Helen sees all of me.

"I think you're a good guy, you know," she tells me softly. "You don't see it, or *want* to see it, but you are."

"I . . . have sex with dead girls."

"And I eat babies."

"I never said you were a good person."

She winces slightly, and it seems like I've offended her. She doesn't appear angry, though . . . just saddened. Like I've hurt her feelings. She bites her lip and looks away. "I should go," she says. "I'll . . . see you around."

Now is the part where I'm supposed to tell her I didn't mean it like it sounded, that to me, being a "good person" is a silly and meaningless moniker, no different than being a "normal person". Society defines what's *good* and what's *bad*, and society doesn't know the difference between its own anal-beaded asshole and its dick-sucking mouth. Fuck being a good person. I'm not a good person because I don't give people enough time or acknowledgment to allow them to define me, one way or another. Labels fucking suck.

Good people fucking suck.

So, yes, this is the part where I'm supposed to tell Helen I like her just fine as she is, which says an awful lot, given the obvious fact that I hate everyone. I'm supposed to explain to her that neither of us needs to be a good person, or *any* kind of person. We just need to be who we are. We just need to fuck dead girls and eat babies and feel good about it.

I'm supposed to tell her all of this, but I don't say anything.

She gives me one more smile, a tiny one this time, and I think there are tears in her eyes. Then she gets out of the car and walks up her long driveway, and into her enormous house.

I drive off to the self-imposed squalor of my home, thinking about what it would be like if Helen was dead.

A few nights later, I'm outside smoking when I hear the automatic doors open behind me. I don't have to look to know who it is.

"Hey," Helen says, coming over to stand beside me.

I hand her a cigarette and light it for her.

"Thanks again for the ride the other night."

"You don't have to keep thanking me. Did you get your car fixed."

"Yes," she says. "My . . . um, someone was able to fix it for me."

"That's good."

We finish our cigarettes in silence. When I turn to go back inside, she stops me, putting a hand on my arm and looking up at me with the light reflected in her glasses. "Listen," she says. "I know you . . . I know it's not your thing, but would you . . . I'd quite like it if you would go to dinner with me sometime."

I look yearningly at the open doors beckoning me away from this absurd request, contemplating making a run for it.

"One dinner, that's it," she persists. "It doesn't have to be a big thing. Just dinner."

My eyes flick from her to the door, and back to her. Back to the door. Back to her. "Listen, I don't go on dates."

"Have you ever actually *been* on a date?"

I'll give you three guesses as to what the answer to this question is. The idea of sitting across from a living girl for a couple hours, while she chatters on about her mundane childhood and her favorite Nicholas Sparks novels has never interested me. I'd just as soon go hotboxing with the porn-quoting, pothead foreigner from high school.

Squirt it in my mouth.

Fuck me with your huge black dick.

Puff, puff, pass.

This causes me to wonder how *my* childhood

stories would be received over filet mignon and glasses of Chianti.

"What makes you think I've never been on a date," I say to Helen.

She laughs. "You're a reclusive hospital security guard, who has sex with dead girls. That doesn't exactly qualify you to be in the running for Cleveland's Most Eligible Bachelor. It's not great material for a winning online dating profile, either."

"Then why do you want to go on a date with me."

"*You're* the one calling it a date, not me. It doesn't have to be a big deal. It's just that . . . I don't know, I can relate to you. I can't relate to anyone else. Maybe I just want to get to know you a little better."

"There's not much to know. And I'm . . . very busy." This last bit comes out forced and weak, *I* wouldn't even believe myself, so I'm not surprised when her face tells me she doesn't buy it, either.

"Please," she says.

I'm reminded of my slutty lab partner, whose sexual services of which I was quite unappreciative. Any other guy would think I'm an idiot for wanting to turn down Helen's proposal, but unlike the college girl, she doesn't seem offended or annoyed by my reluctance. Her expression is, instead, patient and serene. Maybe it's the drugs.

Or maybe she really *can* relate to me.

Shit, wouldn't that be a trip and a half.

"Okay," I say, unable to stop myself from sounding begrudging. My tone doesn't seem to bother her, though, because she smiles and reaches down to squeeze my hand. I flinch a little at this peculiar display of, what, affection? Cordiality? For once, I find myself wishing I knew why humans do these strange little things they do.

"Does tomorrow night work?" she asks, letting go of my hand and taking a small step back, as if she is relinquishing my personal space now that she has gotten what she wanted.

"Yeah," I say. "Tomorrow night is fine." I'm off tomorrow night. I wonder if she had some way of finding this out beforehand. I wonder if I'm being paranoid.

"Great," she says, smiling again. "You know where I live. Pick me up around eight?"

"Okay."

"I assure you, it will be completely casual. I'm not like other women, so I don't need the big romantic fairytale first date."

I wince at the word *first*. "I thought we weren't calling it a date," I say.

"*I* wasn't. *You* started it." Her grin is playful, teasing.

"Look," I say, "I haven't done this before, and I didn't read *The Notebook*. Or *Twilight*. Don't expect too much."

"No expectations, I promise."

"Okay. I'll pick you up at eight." I cough into my fist. "Um, I have to go now. I have to go . . . check the monitors."

"Right," she says, with a knowing smile. "Of course. I'll see you tomorrow."

"At eight."

"Yes."

"Okay."

And that's that. I want another cigarette but I have

to get away; now that it's been made definite, the whole thing makes me nauseous with unease. *Legitimately* nauseous. Once inside, and out of her line of sight, I have to sprint to the bathroom to throw up.

As I'm washing my face in the sink, I'm already thinking of ways to get out of it.

I stick to it. For reasons unbeknownst to me, I'm standing in front of my bedroom mirror, adjusting the knot in my tie.

This is absurd.

Now, I'm not much of an internet guy, but due to my unfamiliarity with the dating scene—*ick*, even the word "dating" makes me feel sickly—I consulted Google earlier today with the search phrase "how to prepare for a dinner date".

As you can expect, there was an intimidating abundance of advice articles, ranging from overly simple, to grotesquely in-depth. I chose the one that seemed the simplest, because I have a limited number of fucks to give in regards to this whole thing.

1. Make reservations.

This part was easy enough. I found a nice-looking restaurant downtown called the Nabokov and made reservations for two at eight thirty.

2. Select an outfit.

The article had all sorts of advice respective to the type of establishment being patronized, and the pictures on the Nabokov's website seemed to fit it into the category of "smart-casual". I selected a plain black shirt, a black tie, a decent pair of black jeans, and the black dress shoes I wear to work.

I realize—sort of for the first time, since I don't usually pay attention to shit like this—that I don't have a single article of clothing in my wardrobe that isn't black.

I don't think she'll mind.

I mean, she eats babies.

As an afterthought, I added my only sport coat to the ensemble, which had been worn on one other occasion, that being my mother's funeral. Gallows humor is alive and well.

3. Apply a modest amount of cologne.

This was a real bitch. I, of course, am not the kind of guy who ever wears cologne, so I was required to make a trip to the Dillard's, in Villa Vista, the uppity shopping district just north of Villa Vida. Seeing no need to drop a couple of hundred dollars on something I would only use once, I just took one of the tiny trial bottles of Versace. The saleswoman kept trying to sell me shit in her annoying saleswoman voice, and I seriously contemplated smashing her face through the glass display counter. But at the end of the day, I'm not a violent creature.

4. Buy her flowers.

I fucking hate flowers. I would have foregone this one, but there's a flower shop down the road from Dillard's, so I figured I'd bite the bullet and just do it, Nike-style. I wanted to get a bouquet of black roses to see how much Helen *really* relates to me, but the crotchety old florist frowned at this request and told me she didn't carry anything like that because it's "too depressing". Stupid oversensitive bitch. I went with the tiger lilies, instead.

There are more steps on the list, but since I'm short on both time and fucks, I finish with my tie, put on my jacket, and leave.

When she answers the door, I look at her and it occurs to me that now is the part where my knees are supposed to go weak, and my breath is expected to catch in my throat, but as much as it pains me to disappoint all you bleeding-heart romantics out there, my knees are fine and the rate of my breathing is undisturbed.

The Hallmark Channel has my condolences.

That's not to say, however, that she doesn't look beautiful, because she does—about as beautiful as any woman with a pulse could hope to look. Her hair falls in cascading golden rivers past her shoulders, the color of her lips is deepened to a dark maroon, and her zombie eyes are heavily shadowed and outlined in black, accentuating their dull haziness. Her white satin dress hangs off one shoulder and stops about midway down her thigh, not short enough to be slutty, but not long enough to be modest. There's a string of pearls around her neck, and a diamond bracelet on her left wrist.

I try not to look at her breasts so I lower my gaze and then wonder if she's wearing underwear. Then I wonder why I would wonder that.

Shifting from one leg to the other, I thrust the flowers out at her and say, "Uh, here."

She smiles and takes them gently. "They're beautiful," she says.

Now is the part where I'm supposed to say something profoundly dumb, such as, *Not as beautiful as you.* But that's really not my style. All of this is already starting to edge uncomfortably toward the realm of stereotype. I think about clichés. I think about track four. I swallow thickly and shove my hands in my pockets.

"Would you like to come in while I put these in a vase?" she asks.

"I guess," I say. Probably not the best way to phrase the response, but she doesn't seem to mind. She smiles again and steps aside, gesturing for me to enter.

The foyer is wide and white, but the massive gold chandelier hanging from the high ceiling casts a glow that makes the walls and floor seem almost yellow.

I'm in someone's house. I can't remember the last time I was in someone's house. I start to sweat.

"Come on in," she says, heading down the hallway. "I have to go to the kitchen to put these in some water."

"No," I say, "I think I'll just wait here." I'm afraid I'll pass out if I attempt to venture further into this unfamiliar dwelling.

"Suit yourself," she says with a lazy smile, and I realize she's *really* high, which sets me a little at ease. "I'll be right back."

As I wait, I stare at my shoes and try to pretend I'm not here. I try to think about anything else but the notion that I'm *standing in someone else's house,* about to actually *go on a date.* But then my mind wanders to the fact that I'll soon be in a restaurant, surrounded by people, and the rate of my perspiration increases.

When she returns a few minutes later, she says in a slow, lazy voice, "You're nervous. Don't be nervous. It's just casual. It'll be fun. Something tells me you don't get out much."

I shrug. She takes my arm and we walk silently to my car. Before I realize what I'm doing, I open the door for her—a minor act of chivalry, of which I didn't know I was capable.

She seems taken aback, too, but pleasantly so; she gives me an appreciative smile and delicately gets in, and I accidentally look down her dress and glimpse the strapless white bra supporting the sloping white hills of her breasts. I think of white elephants, which gets me thinking, of course, about abortion.

Dead babies.

This woman eats dead babies.

My stomach quivers, but not out of revulsion.

I have anxious butterflies as I get into the car.

And I've always fancied myself to be a bit of a sociopath, for fuck's sake.

"If you were going to kill yourself," Helen says, "how would you do it?"

Now, while I *am* unaccustomed to all of this dating shit, I *have* seen movies, and I'm pretty sure this isn't the type of question that's usually asked. At least, not on the first date. I would assume that's more of a third or fourth date type of question. But again, what the fuck do I know.

"I . . . haven't really given it a whole lot of

thought," I say. "I'm not the happiest individual in the world, but I'm more or less content."

She pops a fried squid in her mouth and chews slowly, dead eyes affixed to mine in such a purposeful manner that I'm almost uncomfortable. "I didn't ask you *if* you're going to kill yourself, I asked *how* you would, if you were going to do it. I mean, I'm not going to kill myself, either, but if I were going to, I think I'd hang myself. I know it's a cliché, but there's something kind of poetic about it, don't you think?"

"I don't know how to tie a noose."

She laughs and says, "It's just a slipknot."

"I was never a Boy Scout."

"How about . . . cutting your wrists in the bathtub? They say the hot water prevents you from feeling much pain at all. And watching all that red bloom out of you, surrounding you and engulfing you—I think it would be beautiful."

I think of the girl to whom I'd lost my virginity. I think of Enya.

"Never was into baths. I'm more of a shower kind of guy."

"Pill overdose?"

I shake my head. "I don't like drugs. The strongest thing in my apartment is Tylenol."

She makes a face and says, "You definitely don't want to overdose on *that*. Tylenol overdose is one of the slowest and most painful ways to die. It basically turns your insides to stone. If you don't get your stomach pumped in time, all the doctors can do is watch you die. And that takes about four days. Four days of extreme suffering."

"Well, I guess that's out, then."

"How do you feel about drowning? I read somewhere that people who drown experience an incredible sense of peace and euphoria right before they die."

I raise an eyebrow. "How could they know that. Who is providing testimony for this research."

"Hmm. Good point."

"No drowning for me, euphoria or not. I can't swim."

"If you were drowning, you wouldn't *have* to swim. That's . . . kind of the point."

I shrug. "Whatever."

"Okay, so *think*. Seriously, how would you do it?"

I purse my lips and give the inquiry legitimate contemplation. I could really use a cigarette.

"I wouldn't want it to be clean," I begin. "I would want to leave behind a really nasty, sticky, disgusting mess for whomever found me."

"Mmm, *now* we're talking," Helen says with a grin.

"I guess . . . a shotgun in the mouth would be the most obvious choice. But I think I'd want to do something more creative. I like the idea of, I don't know, crafting a small homemade explosive and then swallowing it. Blow up, from the inside out. Or maybe . . . drenching myself in napalm. You can make that, you know. Equal parts gasoline and frozen orange juice concentrate."

"I know," she says, grin widening. "I read *Fight Club*, too."

"It's one of my favorites."

"*Invisible Monsters* is better."

This new direction the conversation is taking leads

me to believe we might actually veer into more normal waters, which would be both relieving and nerve-wracking—the current topic is pretty intense, but then again, what good have I ever been at *normal?* What good have I ever *wanted* to be?

I realize, then, that she's doing this on purpose. For *my* sake. She's playing into my morbid preoccupation with death, something she's picked up on too quickly for my liking.

But I guess I don't hide it that well, either.

I mean, I fuck dead girls.

I needn't have worried, because she segues into another subject that seems a little deep for a first date. Maybe not necessarily third-or-fourth-date-deep, but second-date-deep, at the very least. From what I would assume, based on my minimal knowledge.

"What do you *want* out of life?" she asks, taking a languid sip of her wine and then leaning slightly toward me. "Tell me your desires. If you could have anything, *do* anything, what would it be?"

I shrug and push my food around on my plate with my overly heavy fork. "Nothing much," I say. "Like I said, I'm pretty much content. I just want to fuck dead girls and not get caught. If I can keep doing that, I'll be fine." There's more to it, but I don't feel like talking about it.

She shakes her head and leans in closer. "No," she says. "That's not true. Everyone wants something more. What are your deepest, darkest fantasies? Don't give me some canned answer. Give me something real. Tell me what you really, truly *want.*"

"More wine, miss?"

This comes from the waiter, who looks perturbed

and uncomfortable, making me wonder how long he's been standing there.

Helen looks up at him with a curt, polite smile. "No, thank you. But a *café con leche* and a cup of masala chai, if you could. Hot."

"Right away, miss," the waiter says, coattails flapping as he spins and hurries off.

I raise an eyebrow at Helen. "Wine, espresso, and tea." It's meant to be phrased inquisitively, but you know by now how I am with that, so it comes out sounding like a bored, bland observation. Which is essentially what it is, anyway.

She seems to understand my being perplexed, because she elaborates by saying, "Yes. I enjoy the finer things in life, and see no reason why one can't indulge in a number of them at once, even if they don't 'go together'."

"Fair enough," I say. The waiter brings her the steaming beverages, and as she's stirring the coffee, I say, "Well, uh, what other 'finer things in life' do you enjoy, besides infantile cannibalism and high-brow drinks."

She shrugs, taking a silver flask from her purse and tipping some of its contents first in the coffee, and then in the tea. "I like Russian literature a lot. Dostoyevsky, Tolstoy, you know. *Real* Russian literature, though, not the bastardized English translations."

"I didn't know you were bilingual."

She sips her tea and shakes her head. "No, not bilingual. Russian was the first foreign language I learned, followed by Latin, then, after that, was Mandarin, then Italian, and finally French, which is my favorite. I can speak some Spanish, but never really studied it. It's such an ugly language, really."

Pushing my food around my plate some more, I say, "I hadn't taken you to be so . . . "

"Intelligent?"

I lower my eyes. "That's not exactly what I meant."

She smiles halfheartedly and pops a couple of pills, washing them down with the last of her wine. "It's okay," she says. "I don't think the general public holds cannibals in very high regard, in any sense of the phrase."

"I'm not representative of the general public."

"True, but you're among them, just as much as I am. We might not be *like* them, but we are still a *part* of them, whether you like it or not."

I bristle at this accusatory statement. "Are you sure that's not wishful thinking on your part."

"It's *realistic* thinking. No matter how much of an individual you are, no matter how unique and different and nonconformist and antiestablishment, you can't deny the inescapable effects that society has on *everyone*, including you and me."

I clench my fists under the table. "No," I tell her, "you're wrong. I'm not part of society. You aren't, either. You just won't accept it."

She looks into her espresso and frowns. For a while, neither of us says anything. I watch her eat a couple bites of her food, and I'm struck again with that sensation of almost-pity for her, because I know she's not really enjoying it. I think back to the blowjob from the college girl, how bland and boring it had felt, and I know that's what she's feeling right now.

I'm relating to another human being.

Hold the phone and shoot me in the fucking face.

I can tell by her expression that I've hurt her feelings again. I could end all of it here, just leave it at my last comment, ask for the check the next time the waiter stops by. Something tells me that's exactly what I should do. Stop all of this nonsensical bullshit, fuck dinner dates and flowers and cologne and worthless chivalry, fuck it all. Stop pretending I'm something I'm not.

Instead, I ask her, "So, um, what kinds of movies do you like to watch."

I have commenced small talk.

She looks up and the cloud of wounded distress seems to clear from her face. She smiles. She knows exactly what I've just done. She knows that I had a clear opportunity there to let it all be over with, but I've salvaged it—stoked the flame, so to speak. I've . . . *made an effort.*

If only she were dead.

None of this would be an issue.

But she isn't.

She's alive.

And something has happened—*is* happening— and it terrifies me.

I pull into her driveway this time, so she doesn't have to walk as far. Color me chivalrous one more time, and then never again.

She turns to look at me as she unbuckles her seatbelt, smiles, head cocked to the side, and says, "Would you like to come in for a drink?"

Now, I have another opportunity here. I can say no, I'm tired, I have to get home. I can just flat-out say it would be inappropriate, that this was supposed to be a casual thing, and I know what the whole "would you like to come in for a drink" thing means. I don't watch much TV, but I watch enough. I can call it a night right here, and that will be that. I, once again, have the chance to end this before it becomes any more ridiculous than it already is.

Instead, I say, "Okay."

I don't open her door for her, though.

Like I said, never again.

She sits too close to me on the couch. She holds her glass of wine with graceful sophistication, while I clutch my glass of water like it's some foreign object, my trembling hand making the ice rattle annoyingly. She's turned on the Gutter Twins' *Saturnalia*. I can't help but be impressed by her taste in music, and this simple fact makes me more nervous.

Helen puts her hand on my thigh, sending a twist of not-unpleasant energy shooting up into my groin, and says, "Try not to be so nervous. It's just me. You know me. Better than anyone, when you think about it."

She says this like it's a good thing. Does all of this sound like a Danielle Steele novel? That's what it feels like, and it makes me want to squirm.

I'm staring at the black bearskin rug in front of the crackling fireplace and wondering if it's real. It doesn't seem to suit her. Neither does the musket hanging above the mantle, or the framed Picasso prints on the wall. I wonder to myself, do I *really* know her?

"I'm not nervous," I say in an unconvincing voice, that cracks on the last syllable. Her hand is still on my thigh. She slides it a little higher and squeezes. I take a sharp intake of breath that I hope she doesn't notice, but I know she does. I sip my water and avoid her alluring gaze of cold, murky deadness.

"It's really not so bad," she says, her tone hushed and buttery. "Being alive. You should give it a chance." She's moved closer, and her breath is warm on my face. I silently tell myself I hate it—her closeness, the proximity of her body starting to envelop me. I tell myself it's horrible. I tell myself to get up and leave. But my inner voice is even less convincing than my outward one.

And then her lips are on mine, and while I don't, at first, reciprocate the kiss, I don't resist it, either. The warmth of her mouth is prevalent, but not unbearable, and the dry taste of the wine is faint enough not to be an issue. She presses the kiss against my upper lip and holds it there, then moves it to my lower lip, and then something tragic happens.

I kiss her back. I move my hand to her hair and push my face against hers. I let the water tumble from my other hand so I can stroke the cool, smooth flesh of her leg. Her wine glass falls, forgotten, to the floor, and its remaining contents stain the carpet like the blood of a devoured infant. Our lips part and our tongues entangle like writhing worms on a rotting corpse. She puts her hand on my crotch and grips it tightly, and I gasp a little into her mouth. I slide my own hand up her leg, to her hip, onto her breast. A rush of blood engorges and stiffens my cock, and she unbuttons my jeans and gently tugs it free. Her grip tightens as she starts stroking it, and I gasp again. I yank her dress down, slide my hand under the cup of her bra, and glide my thumb over her hardening nipple. She lets out a soft moan and then pushes me onto my back, pulling my jeans down, and then I—

And then I'm pushing her off me, heaving myself off the couch and tripping over my pants, which I hastily pull up. I sprint for the front door, bursting out into the night air and dashing down the driveway, holding my maddeningly erect dick in my hand as I run. When I reach my car, I lean against it and finish myself off, stroking myself frenziedly until thick streams of semen spurt out onto the pavement, to the beat of my barbaric grunts.

I see Helen in the doorway, half-naked, mascara tears running down her cheeks, and I get into my car and stab the key at the ignition until it finally slides home and the engine grumbles to life. I throw it in reverse and step on the pedal, tires squealing as the car shrieks down the driveway and swerves onto the street.

I take one more look at her silhouetted figure against the light of the doorway before bursting off into the dark.

The next night, she comes into the security office and sits down. She doesn't say anything. I don't look at her, but I'm shaking.

She pops a couple of pills and starts nervously (I think) pulling at the end of her ponytail. "Listen," she says, and then pauses for a few long beats before saying, "I'm sorry. I'm really, really sorry."

This is unexpected. I'd thought she'd come to demand an apology from *me*, which I suppose would have been justified; I had, after all, abandoned her right in the middle of a pivotal moment of sensuality, directly denying her advances. I don't know how self-esteem works for people, especially women, but I know that couldn't have been good for hers.

"Why are you sorry," I ask.

"I shouldn't have put you in that position. I know . . . what you're like, and how you like to do things. It was sweet of you to take me out, and I can't imagine that had been easy for you. But to come on to you like that . . . it wasn't fair."

"It's whatever," I say uneasily, avoiding her ghostly gaze. "Really, it's nothing. Don't . . . worry about it."

"No, it's *something*, and I *am* worried about it. You're something extremely unique. I see you as a kindred spirit, you know? We were meant to find each other." She's doped up, so I really hope that's where this sentimental bullshit is coming from. "We were meant for each other," she says, "but not as lovers. I don't have friends—not *real* ones, who know the *real* me. I know you don't, either. People intimidate me, and I know they intimidate you, too. Whatever this all is, I don't want to fuck it up. So . . . I'm sorry I tried to have sex with you."

"Okay," I say. "Just don't do it again. Please. Everything will be fine if you just please don't do it again."

"I won't. But I want to make it up to you."

"No. I don't want anything. Stop."

"I want to let you watch me eat."

My heart flutters. I can't even try to tell myself the prospect of that isn't enthralling. When I first discovered her, she'd had her teeth buried in the infant's limp arm, but she'd immediately retracted them when she saw me. I didn't get to see how it started, how it ended, how she chewed or how she swallowed. I've tried to picture it, but to actually *see* *it*—that would be . . . beautiful. The "miracle of childbirth" in morbid reverse. Or something like that.

She doesn't wait for an answer, because she already knows what it will be. "When is your next night off?" she asks.

"Thursday," I say.

"I'll take that night off, too, then. We can go to one of my places, and you can watch me eat."

"You don't have to do that," I tell her. I say it strictly as a formality, and she knows it.

"I want to," she answers, and I know she does. "Pick me up around midnight, okay?"

"Okay."

My heart is beating too fast. My dick is half-cocked, and I fold my hands on my lap, over my groin.

"I have to get going," Helen says, sort of apologetically. "Again, I'm really sorry about last night." She stands up, and as she's going out the door, she looks over her shoulder and whispers, "Thursday."

"Thursday," I whisper back.

Thursday.

"Is this your usual spot," I ask as we trot briskly through the empty abortion clinic parking lot. It's a cold night for July, and I'm shivering a little. Fucking Ohio. Midwest summers don't count for shit.

"Yeah," she says. "There are a couple of other ones that I hit up, but this one is closest."

As we come up to the door, she fishes her key ring out of the pocket of her tight jeans and hands me her bundle of items—a folded white sheet, a couple of washcloths, and a roll of black trash bags. She's got a duffel bag slung over her shoulder. When she slides one of her keys into the lock, I say, "How did you get a key to an abortion clinic."

"I'm the head maternity doctor at a mildly esteemed hospital," she says. "It doesn't count for much, but it counts for enough." She smiles at me as she pushes open the door, and it's a very dead smile; she's been anxiously chewing pills ever since I picked her up, and her heady inebriation is painted all over her face, like the blank canvas of a frustrated artist. I even caught her drooling and nodding off in the passenger seat a few times on the way here. I've never been more attracted to her.

"Apparently so," I say, following her inside. The front door opens into a waiting room that's dark and smells strongly of Clorox and latex. She flips on the light, illuminating uncomfortable-looking plastic chairs, and a small wooden table with a smattering of gossip magazines. As if *Cosmo* is appropriate reading material for a girl who's about to have a kid flushed out of her cunt.

"The basement is this way," she says, with an eagerness that defies her narcotic intoxication. She takes my hand and leads me through another door, down a narrow white hallway decorated with posters proclaiming the importance of safe sex and the proper use of birth control. I feel bad for sad fucks who have to wear condoms. I mean, I don't *actually* feel bad for them, but you know what I mean.

We hurry past some exam rooms, and then she procures another key that grants us access through a heavy steel door emblazoned with a toxic waste sign and the words "WARNING: HAZARDOUS MATERIALS" written underneath it in about eight different languages.

The metal stairs clang under our feet, and I have to hold the handrail to keep from tripping in the darkness. The surety with which Helen proceeds makes me curious as to how many times she's made this descent.

She flips another light switch when we get to the bottom, revealing a square gray room with cement floors and a number of hand-washing stations and huge, padlocked filing cabinets. Along the wall to the left are a handful of garbage bins bearing the same hazardous waste logo. "Is that where they keep the, um, goods," I ask, gesturing at the garbage cans.

She shakes her head. "No, that's just used syringes and gloves and tools and whatnot." She points to a freezer door on the other side of the room and says, "*That's* where the good stuff is." The freezer door is also marked with the toxic sign, but this one only has the "WARNING" message in three different languages. Sorry, Finland.

Helen takes the bundle from me and moves to the center of the room, where she lays out the sheet and sets aside the garbage bags and washcloths. She then looks at me, biting the inside of her cheek, and says, "I'm going to get undressed now."

I'd forgotten about that part.

"Okay," I say. My voice is suddenly hoarse. "I'll . . . turn around."

"You don't have to."

I swallow. "I'm going to, anyway." But I don't. I can't. It's like in dreams, where you try to run but your legs won't listen to your brain, no matter how loud you scream at them to move. I stay rooted in place and look at her. My palms are sweating. My tongue is a dry and unfamiliar obstruction in my mouth; it feels like it's swollen to three times its size and I'm terrified I'm going to choke on it.

Her eyes on mine, gray and unblinking, she pulls her sweater off and lets it fall to the floor.

This shouldn't be a big deal. I've seen her naked before.

She has a figure-hugging white tank top underneath, and she peels that off next, revealing the navel piercing and the hip tattoo I'd forgotten about, as well as a pink bra that seems a little too lacy and erotic for the occasion. I wonder if she did that on purpose.

Her eyes are still locked with mine when she unhooks the bra and tosses it atop the other discarded articles. Her pale nudity, in tandem with the slack, stoned, might-as-well-be-dead look on her face, sends a chill down my back, and a tingling quiver down my cock.

Might-as-well-be-dead isn't the same as *dead*, though, and I have to keep telling myself this to keep an erection at bay. Christ, this is ridiculous.

She steps out of her sneakers and then pulls her jeans and underwear down at the same time, finally tearing her gaze away so she can fold her clothes into a neat little pile. Then she stands back up and resumes staring at me, as if waiting for an appraisal of her naked body.

My hands are shaking as I light a cigarette. "You should get started," I say, my voice barely above a whisper. She nods and turns around to walk over to the freezer. She pulls the door open and then disappears inside, leaving it slightly ajar. Cool air drifts out in silver plumes.

She's still in there when I finish my cigarette, so I crush it out and then drop it into one of the toxic trashcans. I lean against the wall and light another, and then she emerges.

Her hands and forearms are already stained red, and she's holding a shriveled, not-fully-developed fetus. It looks a little too big to be what I would think is abortion-eligible, but hey, what do I know.

"I know what you're thinking," Helen says. "But the best law to ever get passed in Ohio authorizes late-term abortions for extreme scenarios. Usually, abortions don't look anything like this. They're just chopped-up globs of meat. Every once in a while, though, I get lucky and find one that's more or less baby-shaped, like this one. It adds a crucial element to the fantasy." She stares affectionately at the dead thing in her hands as she walks over to sit down in the middle of the sheet she's laid out. She's drooling again. She sniffs it and licks red slime from its misshapen body. A small moan escapes her lips.

This must be what rapture looks like.

I'm not even going to try to describe the sound of her biting into the thing's lopsided head. Just suffice it to say it's kind of jarring. She chews slowly, thoughtfully, and then moans again after she swallows. Pressing her now-maroon lips to the hole she's made in its skull, she noisily slurps out whatever fluids may be floating around in there, before tearing off a sizable chunk of its tiny arm with her scarlet teeth. More moaning, and now she's touching herself, masturbating as she chews. At some point I forget about my cigarette, and it goes out and falls to the floor. I hadn't known about this part of the dining process. Maybe it's for my benefit, but I don't think so. This seems too practiced, too ritualistic. I've heard of women associating sex with food, but I'm pretty sure this is uncharted territory.

"Oh, God, oh, *fuck*," she says through a mouthful of flesh as a clear stream of fluid ejaculates from between the blushing lips of her vagina, while she continues to stimulate herself with her bloody fingers.

She's covered in blood now; it's streaked and dotted across the tops of her breasts, running down between them, and spattered over her face and shoulders. She's still wearing her glasses, and the lenses are freckled with tiny red flecks.

My dick is hard.

She's totally oblivious to me, completely engrossed in her engorgement, and that just makes me harder. Watching her stuff her zombified face with fat chunks of dead fetus while she finger-fucks herself into orgasm after leg-shaking orgasm—I've never been so turned on by a living woman.

With little thought, I'm suddenly approaching her, fumbling with my belt and dropping my pants, tripping a little as I step free of them, my erect cock standing at quivering attention. She's still unaware of me, all the way up until I'm standing over her, with my shadow enveloping her naked figure, and I get on my knees, straddling her pale thighs, and shove her on to her back.

"Yes," she says, dropping the remains of the baby and running her scarlet hands under my shirt. "Yes."

"Keep eating," I tell her as I slide in. "Don't stop. Don't stop eating."

She obeys my command, resuming her feast while thrusting her hips into my pelvis.

Too warm.

Too wet.

Too alive.

That's how I would describe her cunt.

But it's okay, because her face is dead, and the chilled air of the basement renders her skin cool to my touch. I clutch her cold breasts as I fill her with every last inch of my cock. She groans as she gobbles, and I tell her to stop, no noise, just eat. She does, though she has to keep biting her lip to keep from crying out. She squirts a few more times, slickening my groin with sticky vaginal liquid.

I'm able to go for longer than usual, due to the less-than-favorable conditions, but eventually she casts aside the last of the fetus, moans out a nigh-incoherent apology, and then shrieks a shrill orgasmic scream just as I finish inside her. I flop down beside her on the bloody sheet, shaking violently.

Withdrawing my cigarettes from my shirt pocket, I light one and listen to Helen gasp next to me. "I thought . . . you don't like . . . fucking live women," she pants.

"I don't," I say, not looking at her. "There was something different about this."

"Like the fact . . . that I was eating . . . a dead baby?"

"Yeah," I say. "Something like that."

"Do you want . . . to try some of it?"

"I'll pass."

A still, awkward silence falls over us. I smoke tiredly. I've always hated this part. With live women, of course—it's not a problem with the dead ones. Pillow talk has never been my forte. I mean, shit, conversation in general gets me all tense and weird, so I'm entirely incapable of that whole post-coital ruminating on the nature of life and love, or whatever garbage they prattle on about in movies after the obligatory sex scene. I feel like I should say *something*, though, and I'm still trying to think of what exactly that might be when she reaches over and takes my cigarette, sucking hard enough on it for the paper to crackle. She coughs as she exhales, apparently still out of breath.

"I should get dressed," she says, returning the cigarette to my fingers. She doesn't get up, though. She just lies there. I can hear her breathing. I can feel the heat rolling off her perspiring flesh. I can even smell the distinct scent wafting from between her still-parted legs.

I am uneasy and repulsed, but not as much as I should be.

When a few more minutes pass by, and she still hasn't moved, I say, "I'm sorry if I wasn't very good. I'm not used to them . . . moving."

I feel her look over at me, and then she laughs. Kind laughter, light and amused, not mocking. "It was wonderful."

"So you say."

"I don't come like that for everyone."

"So you say."

She rolls over onto her side and props herself up on her elbow. I could tell her it's a stereotypical pose, and that it's not as sexy in real life as it is in the movies, but I don't. "You're being awfully insecure for someone who talks so confidently about being comfortable in your uniqueness," she says.

I don't have anything to say to that.

She looks into my eyes and says, "You need to relax." After a few moments go by and I don't answer, she asks me, "What are you thinking about?" She takes the cigarette again, which annoys me; she keeps wet-lipping it with her bloody lips.

"Nothing," I say, blinking at the ceiling. "I'm not thinking about anything. Sex empties me. It fills my void until it wells up and overflows, and I am consumed by black . . . nothing. It makes me blank."

There's another weird silence, and then she says, "I'm sorry. I know you don't want to talk. If . . . um, you can sleep for a while, if you want."

"I think I will," I say, already drifting. She says something else, but I don't hear it. I'm already gone.

The blood is dry on her naked skin when she wakes me. Her eyes seem more alert, so the pills must be wearing off. I squint through half-lidded eyes at my watch; I've been asleep for about an hour.

"I have something for you," Helen says. "And I want to watch." She's kneeling in front of me and her hands are behind her back.

I'm still fuzzy with sleep, so everything is kind of foggy; if you sleep for longer than twenty minutes, you shouldn't wake up until at least two hours have elapsed or you'll interrupt the REM cycle, and it fucks you up. My head thus feels heavy and cumbersome. My mind is too slow. "What are you talking about," I ask, and it sounds far away. My eyes ache.

She takes her hands out from behind her and presents the "something" in question.

And I'd thought the last one seemed too big to be aborted. "Jesus, Helen. I'm not eating that. I told you already."

She shakes her head, lips stretched across her face in a bloody grin. "I don't want you to *eat* it," she says, and then she touches her finger to the tiny vagina between the fetus's stubby legs. "I want you to *fuck* it. I want you to fuck the shit out of this dead baby."

I regard her, unblinkingly. Now, I've fucked corpses across all age ranges, with the oldest being in her late fifties and the youngest being nine, but *this*—this is weird, even for me. "Helen, I don't know . . . that's really not my style."

Balancing the fetus on one hand, she runs the other down my stomach and cups my testicles. Her grip is ice cold. I stiffen immediately.

"*There* you go," she coos. "Now, go ahead, lie

down." She gently pushes me onto my back and then mounts the fetus atop my erection. The dead infant's cunt is cold and slightly hard, but the tightness is unlike any girl I've ever fucked before.

"Mother*fuck*," I breathe, reaching down and wrapping my hands around its tiny waist. Helen is beaming and masturbating as I start to bob the kid up and down, its head lolling around with its mouth open and its tongue hanging out. I thrust harder and I can feel its insides tearing. I clench tighter and my fingertips punch through its flesh.

Helen is kissing my neck with cold lips and digging her fingers through my hair.

My penis is all the way up in the baby's stomach, blending its insides into a pulpy slop. "This is so—oh God, oh God—fuck, this is so fucked *up*," I groan.

The skin on the baby's neck has ripped and its head is about halfway dislodged, so I have to put one hand on its soft scalp to keep it from detaching completely. The thing is falling apart in my hands, but it just feels so fucking good.

Helen gets up and sits on my face, so I start tonguing her and she cries out as a rush of fluid floods my mouth. Not exactly my thing, but I do have a dead baby on my dick, so one could argue tonight is all about exploring new areas. I use my free hand—as in, the one that's not holding the baby's head on—to fondle Helen's breasts as she grinds against my mouth, her pubic stubble tickling my chin. The extent of her cries should piss me off, but all I can think about is the deliciously tight cunt enveloping my cock, which feels ready to burst at any moment but hasn't yet, mercifully prolonging the ecstasy.

I lose my grip on the head and I feel it peel off and tumble onto my stomach, so yes, I am now fucking a *headless* dead baby, thank you very much.

I'm breathing heavily through my nose, and I keep having to swallow Helen's endlessly flowing juices. Her nipple is hard against my palm, and my other hand is tearing new holes in the fetus's skin as I struggle keep hold of it, to prevent it from flying off. Just when I'm thinking it's about to slip from my grasp and go soaring into the air, my abdomen is wrenched by the most blindingly intense orgasm I've experienced in the entire freakshow of my life, and I scream an animal cry of pleasure into Helen's gushing vaginal canal. I can feel globs of semen seeping out of the holes in the baby's now-mangled corpse, and finally it *does* fly off, and I hear it thud squishingly on the floor, a few feet away, in between Helen's shrieks. The tip of my penis is still spurting, and I claw at Helen's back with my newly freed hand.

I shove her off me when I'm done, gasping hoarsely, my cheeks damp and sticky with her copious ejaculate. "Fuck me *sideways*," I say wheezily. "That was fucking unbelievable."

"I've . . . never done anything like that before," Helen says from beside me. "I didn't know sex could be like that."

"I didn't know anything could be like that," I say. I sit up and look at the mess around us, covering us, and at the mashed-up dead baby lying on the floor. "We should probably clean this all up. Some of it got on the floor. The sheet didn't catch all of it."

"I'll bring a bigger sheet next time," she says with a grin, reaching over and squeezing my cock.

"No," I say firmly, grabbing her wrist and moving her hand away. "There won't be a next time."

She's silent for a moment, and then she nods and gestures over at her duffel bag. "I have cleaning supplies in there that I always bring, just in case. I'll fold up the sheet and put it away."

"We should clean ourselves off, first."

"We could clean each other."

"No."

She nods, so we wipe ourselves down with rags, individually, and then get dressed and finish cleaning up the evidence of our presence. She folds the sheet and tucks it into the duffel bag with the cleaning supplies.

We're standing outside my car. I don't know why we haven't gotten in yet. We're just looking at each other.

The way she looks in the moonlight, clichéd beauty to a damning fault, flaxen hair rendered the white gold of karats unmeasurable, eyes glittering like newly-minted silver dollars, burning with feverish yearning, intensified by the thick lenses of her glasses . . . her skin glows, smooth ivory polished to the white purity of new snow, and all I can say is, "I wish you were dead."

She blinks slowly, shutters swinging closed over the windows to her shuddering soul, only to be flung back open once more, piercing through to my own inner self, and she says, "Sometimes *I* kind of wish I were dead."

"You would be perfect."

"Maybe everything else would be, too."

We stand there for a few more moments, and then I drive her home. Not a word is spoken between us the whole way there. I don't tell her goodbye. She just looks at me for a second, and then she leaves. I don't watch her as she walks up the driveway.

Some nights I go to the graveyard because it's always been the only place where I can truly relate to people.

Morgues are great and all, but none of those people have been dead more than a couple of days. I've been dead inside for a long time. When I dream of camaraderie, I'm surrounded by skeletons, flesh barely clinging to their ancient bones.

Helen, though.

Helen is alive.

This poses a problem for me.

It's warm outside and my hands are in my pockets as I stroll through the rows of headstones. There's a light breeze and the moon is bright behind the canopy of rolling gray clouds. It smells like impending rain. I tread lightly, out of respect, because I think the long-dead sleep a fitful and restless slumber, and I'm preoccupied with my thoughts, so it's more important than ever not to stir them.

Despite the night's warmth, I am cold. There's this chilly feeling you get in graveyards. You don't really feel it come on—it just happens, to the point where you're enjoying the warm whisper of a summer wind and then, all of a sudden, you realize you're cold. It's a strange kind of cold—it's sort of an icy tingling that starts at your shoulders, around the base of your neck, and it permeates through your veins in place of your blood. It's like the kind of chill you get when you have an eerie realization, or experience a joltingly bizarre coincidence. That "someone just walked over my grave" feeling. Someone get me a snare drum.

The difference, though, is it *lingers*. Most "ooh, I've got chills" moments last but only a few seconds. The graveyard chill, however, stays with you until you leave. You don't feel it pass any more than you feel it come on. After you've left the domain of the dearly departed, you're walking away with a serene sense of peace, humbled by ancient dates and pretty stone structures, and then it occurs to you that the chill has disappeared and the mental perception of your body temperature has returned to normal. Everything is as it was, and it's as if time had stood still.

But sometimes, you take one last glance over your shoulder, and though there's never anything there, you'll get one final jolt of the chill, alarmingly potent in its presence, and then it's gone, and you're still alive, and you take comfort in the deceptive notion that, with your back to the cemetery, death is behind you, and not waiting patiently ahead.

But not me.

I live for that chill.

I want death neither behind, nor ahead, of me, but *around* me and *within* me.

Helen, though.

Helen is alive.

Helen is *warm*.

I fucked Helen, and I enjoyed it.

I think I might actually fucking *like* Helen.

Problems, problems.

As I'm lighting a cigarette, I notice a man sitting at a gravestone a few rows ahead, a bottle of liquor lying beside him in the dirt. He's weeping, talking to someone named Roxanne, as if she's really there. Maybe she is; I'm not one to know these things. I give him a wide berth as I pass, and he doesn't see me. A crow cries from one of the black trees.

Helen is alive.

That's all I can think about.

The living are dangerous. They inflict pain. They're so fueled by greed, a lust for useless material shit, a smoldering desire to *fit in* . . . and they'll hurt and betray and destroy whomever they must in order to get anywhere close to all of it. None of them are any different. Not even Helen, really. She craves conformity, longs to be one of the rest.

She *does* eat babies, though. She's got that going for her, at the very least.

But . . . she's alive.

I think of her warm, living flesh, the hot blood coursing through her veins, heart thudding beneath her breasts, and my first thought is . . . *eww*.

But then I realize my dick has engorged itself into a burgeoning erection that struggles against the black denim of my jeans. I try to think about something else, anything else, but naturally my thoughts turn to that night in the abortion clinic, and I fear I'm going to mess myself, so I hastily pull it out and start stroking furiously, thinking of Helen's strong thighs clenching my waist, her glassy eyes rolling up into her head as she cried out in orgasm. In a few moments I'm shooting creamy globs of ejaculate onto the nearest headstone. Sorry, Allan Griswold Clemm, beloved husband and father, January 19th, 1809 to October 7th, 1849. Taking great gulping breaths, I sit down against the one next to it, picking up the cigarette I'd dropped and relighting it.

When, I wonder, is the last time I'd masturbated while fantasizing about a live girl, instead of a dead one?

Sitting there smoking, my flaccid dick hanging out from the open zipper of my jeans, I think to myself, *I could really be in a lot of fucking trouble.*

The death smell seizes me while I'm on one of my rounds and leads me to the doorway of a dim room with floral curtains open to a view of the nigh-empty parking lot. There is no moon, no stars, only the glow of the tall streetlamps.

Lying in the white bed is a young man, late twenties, hairless and covered in tattoos—the kind of tattoos that make mothers hold their children to them and veer the other way. The kind that disqualify you from having any sort of respectable occupation, whatsoever. The bold swastika on his forehead, the inverted pentagrams on his cheeks, the gruesome pictures and designs up and down his pale arms—his body is a canvas of savage and frightening imagery, the cover of a Cannibal Corpse album that never was.

Hunched in the chair beside the bed is a middle-aged priest with thinning black hair, clasping a rosary in one hand, and a weathered bible in the other. He's whispering soothingly to the young man, speaking softly under his breath, words I cannot hear.

"Father Benway," the man interrupts, "I'm scared. I feel it coming."

"Fear not the Angel of Death, my child," says the priest. "She is gentle. She will deliver you peacefully into the arms of Christ."

"What if I don't go to Him? What if I go to hell? All those bad things I've done, Father. I've hurt so many people. I've raped. I've . . . killed."

The priest straightens and covers the young man's hand with his own. "My son, when you made your vows this afternoon, did you speak truly? Were your promises from the heart? Do you reject the sins of your past, and accept Jesus Christ as your Lord and Savior?"

What a load of bullshit.

If I was capable of laughter, this is the part where I'd burst into gales of it.

"Yes, Father Benway," the man says, his eyes big and doleful, brimming with tears. "Yes, yes, I *did* mean it. I'm sorry for everything I've done. I want to go see Jesus now."

It's a queer thing, what death does to people. It makes them say ridiculous things they think they mean. I'm quite sure this man believes he has turned over a new leaf, that he regrets his past, that he is now a man of God, and thus, he will be welcomed through that pearlescent gateway of fabled lore, this prodigal son-of-Satan-wannabe. But if a doctor were to come in here now and tell him there had been a mistake with the prognosis, that he wasn't going to die after all, this neo-Nazi loser would be up and out the door, on his way to find the nearest rally.

Death is funny like that.

"You *will* see Him, child," the priest assures him. "I can see the change in you. I can see the light. The blood of Jesus is upon you."

For fuck's sake.

Neither of them has noticed me yet, but even in the dim light, I can see something in the priest's face, something that gives me a surprising jolt of satisfaction; he doesn't believe what he's saying. He knows he's selling a line of bullshit to this kid. I can't tell how deep his skepticism runs, can't decipher whether he's "lost his faith", or if he really believes his doctrine, but thinks this guy is fucked.

It doesn't matter. There's nothing for me here. I'll see this guy's corpse downstairs in the morgue soon enough, but it will just be part of the audience, in the background, irrelevant.

Not drastically different, I suspect, from its living counterpart.

Call him evil, label him a monster, brand him a menace to society, whatever. He's not so different from your suburban PTA moms, your corporate office drones, your own goddamn kids, even. Everyone's a parasite, each a small part of a collective plague upon the planet. Somewhere, there might be some uninteresting plot to destroy the world, but I don't think so. I don't think they even know they're doing it. They all just exist, with specific roles, not so different from the next.

This young man, like so many others, is here for one purpose.

To die.

The priest is here to make people believe dying really isn't so bad, that there's something on the other side. He's here to make dying easy. To make it attractive.

And me?

I just fuck dead girls.

I go outside for a cigarette, and there's a raccoon by the trashcan. It's eating some small, hairless animal, probably a baby opossum, standing on its hind legs and cradling the thing in its tiny, hand-like paws. It looks up at me, eyes glowing, red innards hanging from the sides of its mouth, but instead of scurrying off, it buries its snout back in the stomach of the dead animal and resumes eating.

I sit on the curb and watch it as I smoke.

Helen's sitting in the security room with me while I stare listlessly at the monitors and try not to look at her, just kind of watching her in my peripheral. Her hair is tied back with a black bow, and she's wearing a new pair of glasses.

"It doesn't have to be like this," she says after a lengthy period of awkward silence.

"Like what," I ask.

"Like *this*. All, you know, *weird* and *uncomfortable*, or whatever it is right now. It's . . . not like it used to be."

"We fucked. Of course it's not like it used to be."

"Nothing's changed. We just . . . had fun, that's all.

It was a fun night, and we can move forward from there. It doesn't have to be a big deal."

"I don't have fun. I have moments of satisfaction in between long bouts of plain existence. That's it. I don't even know what fun is."

She bites her lip and tilts her head sideways. She says, "Okay, well, did you experience a moment of satisfaction?"

I don't answer because both of us know I don't have to answer. I feel trapped, a rat in a cage, a cornered animal, but with less aggression.

"It can't happen again," I tell her.

"Okay. That's fine." There's something in her face that suggests she doesn't mean it.

"I fuck dead girls. Not live ones."

"Okay," she says again.

For a while neither of us says anything else. I watch people go about their normal routines on the monitors, and I can feel her watching me.

"You know," she says eventually, "you never did answer my question on our date."

"What question."

"I asked you what you wanted out of life. Your hopes and dreams."

I tense up. I, for reasons that should be pretty clear by now, never discuss details about things like this. With anyone. But Helen's pushy.

"No," I say cautiously, "I guess I didn't."

"You're in school, right?" she asks.

"Yeah," I say.

"For what?"

I'm quiet for a moment, not wanting to have this conversation. "Business management," I tell her.

"That doesn't sound like your type of field."

"No, it doesn't," I say, hoping she'll stop talking about it.

She doesn't take the hint (or maybe she does, but doesn't care), and she says, "What do you plan to do with it?"

Giving her another chance to drop it, I shrug and say, "What does anyone ever plan to do with a college degree."

"Most people have some sort of ideal occupation."

"I guess," I say, shrugging again. She doesn't say anything, apparently determined to drag this out of me. I sigh. "I want to open a business," I tell her.

"What *kind* of business?"

"A funeral parlor."

She doesn't answer, and I swivel to look at her, trying to read her reaction. She's biting her lip, looking, strangely, like she's about to cry. Instead, she explodes into laughter. "That's *fantastic*," she says, wiping at her eyes with her middle and forefinger. "I mean, it makes *sense*. I've always wanted to open an abortion clinic, but it doesn't really work like that."

"No, I don't suppose it does."

She interrupts the awkward silence that follows by saying, "I wish you'd reconsider. I don't want that night to have been . . . the only time."

"No," I say, my shoulders suddenly tensing up. She won't let it die. I don't know how to be any clearer with her. I grit my teeth and clench my fists and say again, "No."

She frowns. "What's it going to take to convince you? I know I'm not exactly your type, being that I have, you know . . . "

"A heartbeat," I say for her.

"Right. But it was *good*, what we did. It had been a long time since I'd had sex."

"No," I say again.

"I know you want it, too. I can see it in the way you look at me."

I turn back to the monitors. "It was an isolated circumstance. It can't happen again. I told you that right after it happened."

"Yes, well, I didn't think you *meant* it."

"I did. And I do."

She clasps her hands on her lap, looks down at them, shifts in her seat. "Well," she says quietly, not looking up, "if you change your mind . . ."

"I won't."

She nods. I would think this would be the end of it, but it's not. "You're not dead, you know," she says firmly. "Sometimes I think you want to be, but you're not. Everything in your life is about death, but *you* are *not* dead. I don't think you realize that. You're not dead."

"I might as well be."

"What does that even mean?"

"I don't know."

We're quiet for awhile. Then I look at the floor and say, "That night, you said you wished you were dead. You're not really in a place to give this kind of lecture."

Sighing, she says, "I think what I said was that *sometimes* I wished I was dead. I think that's probably true of anyone. Besides, I was emotional." She sighs again. "Listen," she says, "you'll have your chance at death. You'll have a whole eternity of chances. But you only get one chance at life, and it's a very small window."

I snort. "That's original."

"Don't be like that."

"Like what."

Her pager goes off. She glances at it and gets up. "I have to go."

"Okay."

"If you change your mind . . . " she says again.

"I won't," I say again.

She leaves, and I watch her go as soon as her back is turned.

I'm in the morgue, leaning against the wall and smoking, not really horny, but needing to be around dead people.

I think of my dream of owning a funeral parlor. It seems distant, almost surreally so, but I know I can't spend the rest of my life fucking corpses in a hospital basement, as much as I'd like that to be the case.

Sooner or later, I'd get caught.

Helen got caught. She's just lucky I was the one who caught her.

A shudder goes down my spine as I think of her in the state in which I'd found her—naked on her sheet, covered in blood, holding the half-eaten dead baby in her arms like some fucked up anti-abortion ad. Or a *pro*-abortion ad, depending on the kind of shit that tickles your fancy.

As I look over the covered bodies, I think of horror movies, where they sit up and start walking around. If that happened, they'd be able to fuck me back.

Like Helen had.

Like Helen *could*, if I so desired.

The *point*, though, is for them *not* to fuck me back. Isn't it?

I take out my cell phone, turning it over in my palm. I don't get any service down here, but I could go upstairs and call her. I don't remember when she gave me her phone number, but I have it, and I know she's not working tonight. She'd answer on the second ring, maybe the third, voice sleepy but alert. I'd tell her I want to come over, and she'd ask how soon I could get there.

No.

I have to stop thinking like this.

If I'm not careful, everything I've built within myself could unravel. My solitary mind palace, composed of every dead girl I'd ever fucked, would come crashing down. I'd suddenly be . . . *one of them*.

The normal people.

The people who have real sex with other humans, *living humans*.

I've always stayed true to myself—to my unique passion—and because of that, I've remained safe, untouched. If I start to become like all the other flea-ridden sloths of this country, I'll become vulnerable, stripped bare, unprotected against the elements. I am fortified by that which makes me different. As long as I remain on the outside, on the lunatic fringe, if you will, I cannot be harmed. But if I allow Helen to pull me into the swarming mass of walking, talking, slobbering trolls, I'll instantly be trampled.

I just can't have that.

I put my phone back in my pocket and jerk off into a trashcan.

Helen tells me I need more light in my life.

We're standing on her porch; I had to drive her home because her car wouldn't start again. I walked her to the door because I think that's what I'm supposed to do. *Not* chivalry. Just . . . I don't know, a weak attempt at politeness, I guess.

I ask her, "What light." I ask her where it is.

She says, "Everywhere."

I tell her no, and she says I have to look for it. I look at my shoes and say quietly, "I can't see, anyway. I really can't see anything at all."

"Don't you *want* to see?" she asks.

"No," I say, looking up and meeting her gaze. "No, I really don't." She starts to speak. I cut her off. "Your problem," I say, "is that you spend too much time running from your own darkness. You should accept it. Embrace it. Hide in it, instead of hiding from it."

"What's so bad about the light?"

"You can see better. And most things aren't worth looking at."

She reaches up and unties her ribbon, shaking her hair out. I'm not sure why.

"I don't think I have as much darkness as you do," Helen says. "Or as much darkness as *you* think I do."

"You eat babies," I say. "You have plenty of darkness."

She frowns and puts the ribbon in her pocket and then opens her front door. It wasn't locked. "Do you want to come in?" she asks hopefully.

Maybe that's why she shook her hair like that.

Some sort of human mating ritual that's supposed to induce arousal. It doesn't work.

"No," I say. "I have to go."

"To check the monitors?" she says tauntingly.

"Yeah," I say. "To check the monitors."

The janitor and I are outside smoking when an ambulance pulls up under the awning. Its flashers turn off, the back doors open, and three paramedics file out hurriedly. Despite their rushed urgency, their faces are calm, shoulders relaxed, their movements quick but languid.

They pull out a gurney and there's a man on it, looking to be about my age, but in worse condition—he's covered in blood and puke. The bleeding seems to be coming from his nose, but it's hard to tell. He's raving about some girl named Vera. I think of that Pink Floyd song on *The Wall*. A blonde girl gets out and stands close to the gurney, face wrought with concern. She's not Vera. I don't know how I know this.

Two of the paramedics wheel the gurney inside with the blonde girl closely in tow. The third paramedic hangs back and asks the janitor for a cigarette. The janitor complies, and the paramedic lets him light it for him. He leans back against the ambulance and runs a hand through his hair.

"What happened to him?" the janitor asks.

"Alcohol poisoning and drug overdose," says the paramedic, as he lets the smoke roll from his lips. "Coke and pills, it looks like. Lots of it." He shrugs. "He'll probably die."

The janitor shakes his head sadly and tosses away his cigarette. He sticks his hands in the pockets of his gray coveralls and says, "These kids, I don't get it. All the drugs. Why? What's it doing for them?"

The paramedic shrugs again. "Who knows? It seems like every night we've got some idiot who's OD'd on one thing or another. It's usually heroin, so this guy is a nice change of pace. Fucking morons, though, the whole lot of them."

"I don't think they're morons," I say, surprising myself by speaking. The two of them look at me as if they're just now realizing that I'm here. "If people want to do drugs, let them do drugs. Who are we to judge." I'm thinking of Helen. Helen and all of her pills. The pills that give her the eyes that I so adore. The dead eyes. The eyes of a ghost.

"If you saw some of the shit that I've seen," says the paramedic, "I think you'd feel differently."

"I doubt it," I tell him dismissively. "People all have something that gives them pleasure. What makes doing drugs any different than golfing, or collecting stamps." *Or fucking dead girls. Or getting raped. Or eating babies.*

"I like watching Boris Karloff movies," says the janitor. "And collecting Boris Karloff figurines. And posters and such. But that isn't going to kill me. Drugs kill people."

I crush my cigarette beneath the heel of my boot and light another. "What the fuck do you care who lives or dies," I say. "If that guy in there dies tonight, how will your life be any different."

The janitor opens his mouth to respond but apparently can't think of anything, so he clamps it shut. The paramedic is looking at me like I'm crazy. Maybe he can see inside me and he knows what I am, like Tamara the Rape Girl had. Or maybe he's just a narrow-minded, ignorant imbecile who's been sufficiently brainwashed by society.

Three guesses upon which option I lay my money.

"And if he dies," I continue, "he's winning. He'll go out doing what he loves. I can't think of a better way to go, honestly." I picture Tamara getting beaten and stabbed and gang-raped and loving it. I imagine Helen choking to death on a hunk of baby meat and experiencing erotic asphyxiation as she goes. I envision myself having a massive coronary as I reach the cusp of an orgasm while fucking some dead teenage cheerleader. I look harshly at the janitor and say, "Wouldn't you want to die by having a stroke while jerking off to *Frankenstein*. Forgive the bad pun. Couldn't resist."

"Hey, man," the janitor says, putting his hands up. "Chill out. Don't say shit like that."

The paramedic is snickering, although I'm not sure at what. I've been talking too much. I've engaged myself in these people's lives, and that's bad. You know how I am, by now. I try to be a phantom, just kind of floating through the world, my presence not really registering in anyone's mind. I try to be bland and forgettable. My occasional hallway conversations with the janitor are always brief and in passing, not of any real substance, something he'll forget about as soon as he walks away. That's how it should be. But now I've opened myself up, to a degree, and made my presence known. The janitor will remember this conversation the next time I see him. He must now be avoided.

I . . . have . . . opened . . . up.

How did this happen.

I already know the answer to that as soon as the question enters my mind.

Helen.

Fucking Helen.

Literally.

Has Helen penetrated me and somehow made me more a part of the world? I think about what she keeps saying about "the light". I look at the light overhead. I'm standing in the radius of its illumination. Usually, I stand out of its reach, in the shadows. Shrouded. But here I find myself, for the moment having emerged from darkness, and both men's eyes are on me. They can see me, and I can see them. *Really* see them, for the grotesque, inane chimps they are. I know this of them, of all of them, but I ignore it as best I can so as to avoid nausea and subsequent vomiting.

I am not one of them. I do not want to be among them.

I take a step back, away from the light, back into the shadows, toward the door. I'm suddenly nervous, my body anxiously attempting to claw its way out of my skin. My vision fades, and I'm afraid I might faint.

"It doesn't matter," I tell them, still backing toward the door. "I have to go. I have to . . . check the monitors."

The paramedic tries to say something to me, but I'm already gone, through the doors, thinking back to a similar scenario I'd been in with Helen, not long ago.

And I'm thinking that I wish she were here.

And that's just fucking gross.

She shows up later, not long after my conversation outside. She doesn't even knock anymore. She just comes in and plops down in the extra chair and starts talking. It should annoy me, but it doesn't, and *that* annoys me.

"You don't look so good," she tells me, crossing her legs and twirling a lock of hair around her forefinger. She's really high tonight. There's hardly anything in her face at all. Her eyes are as vacant as the tip jar at the Bad Seed. I think of Nick, the junkie bartender, and figure the two of them would get along nicely.

"What do you mean," I ask, swiveling toward the monitors so I don't have to see her looking at me.

"You look . . . out of sorts. And kind of sick."

"I ate a bad . . . cheeseburger."

"You don't eat cheeseburgers."

"How would you know."

I can feel her smiling her dopey, stoned smile. "You don't seem like the type who eats cheeseburgers."

"You don't seem like the type who eats babies."

"Oh, that reminds me," she says, her voice raising a little, like she's excited about whatever she's just remembered. "I had a dream last night. A good one, this time. Most of them have been bad lately."

"That's . . . good to hear." I don't have to ask her to tell me about it because I know she's going to anyway. She always does.

"I was delivering a baby," she says dreamily, and

when I glance at her she's staring off into space, wearing a crooked grin. "There were other doctors there, too, though. And then the other doctors and I turned into monsters. We ripped open her vagina and pulled the baby out, and we ate it. All of us, we shared it. And I kept thinking, in my dream, that it felt *good*. Not just the baby-eating part . . . the part about all of us doing it. I felt like we were all superior beings. We, the monsters, were special and unique. The mother of the child, and the baby itself—they were nothing. They weren't like *us*."

I start to ask her if I was one of the monsters, because that would make sense, but then she says in her pensive, distracted voice, "The baby's name was Caesar. I don't know how I knew that, but that's what it was. Caesar. And all of us . . . we ate little Caesar. He was delicious."

"That sounds like a very nice dream," I say, because I can't think of anything else.

"It was," she says. "It was very nice. You know, I think . . . I think I'm starting to look at things differently."

"What do you mean."

"I mean, all my life, I just wanted to be normal. But I think I'm starting to see things the way you see them. Maybe it is like you said—we're *special*. To hell with everyone else. People like us, people who are into strange things, I guess—we're better. Than the others, I mean. The *normal people*. They're missing out."

"Yeah," I say. I'm thinking again of Tamara Jericho, who was also into some really strange things, and how she had died so peacefully. Helen would have liked her, I think. We could have been one big happy family of fucked-up weirdos. A group of doctor-monster-things eating a kid named Caesar.

"Anyway," Helen says, "I have to get back to work. I just wanted to stop by. You should take some Tums, or something. You really look awful."

"Yeah," I say again. "Yeah, I'll do that."

I'm not going to take any fucking Tums.

"Listen," she says, pausing on her way out the door, "when I get off, do you want to come over and—"

"No," I say, my sweating hands clenching the armrests of my chair. "No, I don't."

She doesn't say anything else, and I don't watch her leave. I wait to hear the door close, and when it does, I turn and look at it and wonder what I'll say if it opens again, if she comes back and asks me one more time.

She doesn't, though.

The door stays closed.

As it should.

Things go on like that for a while. She comes in and talks to me and tells me her dreams, asks me to interpret them. I never do. Occasionally she tries to get me to come over. I never do that, either.

Then, abruptly, she stops showing up. A couple of nights go by, then a week, then a whole month. I watch her on the monitors, but I don't seek her out. She never goes out to smoke, which I suppose makes sense because, now that I think about it, she only smoked with me, and she never had her own cigarettes.

She's not at the hospital as often. A lot of nights I'll flip through all the cameras in the hospital, even the ones in places she wouldn't have any reason to be, and she's not there.

Something feels off.

I feel off.

Another month passes. September is drawing to a close, but it's savagely, unseasonably hot. Every time I go out to smoke at night, I come back in sweating.

It's toward the end of my shift, and I'm reading *The Sweet Smell of Psychosis* when I'm startled by a knock at the door. I look at the monitor, and it's Helen. I bite the inside of my cheek and think. This is peculiar; she's been absent for over a month, so the visit in itself is strange, in addition to the fact that she's knocking, because she had *stopped* knocking awhile back.

I get up and let her in, and we both sit down. We stare at each other, not speaking, and she looks different. She's gained weight—not much, but enough to be noticeable. Her face seems more flushed, even though her eyes are still dead. She shakes a few pills into her hand and tosses them into her mouth.

"I don't have anything to drink," I tell her. "I already drank all my water. My shift is over soon."

She nods and grindingly crunches the pills down, swallows, and keeps looking at me.

"Where have you been," I ask.

She sighs deeply, her shoulders raising high and then falling low, so she becomes hunched, almost like a scared child. Her shaking hands are clasped on her lap, and her knuckles are white. "Life has become complicated for me," she says.

"Wasn't it always complicated."

Her pale eyes well up. "It's different, now."

"What do you—"

"I'm pregnant."

At that second word I seize up. My heart plummets into my groin, and my blood turns to cold, brown slush. My vision becomes gray, and I fear I'm going to pass out. I take tight hold of the arms of the chair and close my eyes, waiting for it to pass.

Pregnant.

Pregnant.

PREGNANT.

Once I'm reasonably sure I can maintain consciousness, I open my eyes. "It's not mine," I say.

"It is," she says. Tears are now running down her ruddy cheeks.

"No."

"Yes. You're the only person I've had sex with in months. Me and . . . I haven't had sex in a long time."

"How long have you known," I ask.

She shrugs and looks at her lap, appearing again as a frightened child. "A while," she says.

"Why didn't you tell me," I say, trying to make the anger within me evident in my voice. And then, the more important question. "Why haven't you aborted it," I ask.

She makes eye contact with me. "I can't. I won't."

"It is a monster. The way it was conceived . . . it is an abomination."

Her face grows even redder as she says bitterly, "You don't think that *you're* a monster. *You're* the one who's always preaching about being different."

Running a hand through my hair and looking at

the ceiling, I say quietly, "Helen. I don't preach about anything. And just because I'm okay with being me, doesn't mean I think there should be more of me. There should not be more of me. You have to kill it."

"No."

"I hate kids, Helen. I hate them. Flush it out."

"No."

"You eat babies. You don't give birth to them, or raise them."

She bites down hard on her lip and closes her eyes. She's holding back an outburst of sobs. She says, carefully and deliberately, "It's different this time. This time, it's mine."

"It's ours," I correct her. "I have a say in it. And I want it dead."

"It's *my* body," she argues. "Listen, I don't want you to think I came here to tell you that I want anything from you. I don't expect you to be a father, or anything. Obviously, I'd never come after you for child support. You don't have to do anything at all. I just thought you should know about it."

"I want it dead," I say again. I'm panicking. I'm short of breath, and yet horribly craving a cigarette. I close my eyes and massage my temples as I feel a headache begin to settle in, burrowing itself into my skull and building a thorny nest. Helen asks me if I want any of her Vicodin, and I tell her no, I don't want any fucking Vicodin.

"I'm sorry," Helen says. "At first I wasn't going to tell you at all. Maybe I *shouldn't* have told you. But I really think you should know about it, at least."

I meet her gaze and feel the anger leave my eyes and be replaced with pleading desperation. "Please,

Helen," I beg her, somewhat satisfied with the audible amount of anguish I'm somehow able to infuse into my voice. "Please, don't do this to me."

"I'm not doing anything," she says, her tone soft and soothing and motherly. "It's okay, really. It's not even that big of a deal."

I try another approach and say, "You're going to eat it. You know you will. You won't be able to resist it. You're going to eat your own baby, and then you're going to go to prison." As an afterthought, I throw in a little flattery and add, "You're too pretty for prison. The women in there . . . I think they'd eat you alive."

She smiles sadly. "I'm not going to eat my baby," she says. "It's *mine*. I will love it and raise it and everything will be fine."

"Nothing will ever be fine if you have that baby."

"I have to go," she says, standing up. "I'll . . . I guess I'll talk to you later, or something."

"Yeah," I say, swiveling away from her direction. "Or something."

My hands are shaking and my heart is racing as I drive home that morning. I take side roads to allow myself time to think.

It seems clear I won't be able to convince her to abort the fucking thing. Regardless, I can't let it be born. The thought of having offspring, a child with my genes, walking around in the world . . . I can't have that. Some nasty fucking infant with *my* blood lying there and shitting itself and crying like a gutted dog, its ugly little face all scrunched up, squirming and wailing for Helen's tit—I can picture all of it, and it's fucking disgusting. I can't be responsible for bringing another goddamn human onto this godforsaken rock. I try to have as little impact on the world as possible, to leave no trace of my presence, but reproduction is the exact antithesis of that.

I make a right turn into the Metroparks, which typically have little-to-no traffic this time of morning, and which have an exit right onto Jubilee Street. I take this way occasionally; it's quiet and serene, and while I'm not one for the aesthetic appeal of nature, there's something about the way the dawn sun peeks through the canopy of the trees and casts a golden-red light over the road that makes the drive feel almost dreamlike.

I've only been on Parkway Road for about five minutes before I come upon a small gray Ford off to the side of the road, its front end wrapped around an enormous tree, with pale smoke billowing out from under the hood. There are skid marks on the road— the driver had likely been attempting to avoid a deer, I imagine. The evasive maneuver clearly failed in execution.

I pull over about thirty feet behind the crashed car and turn my hazards on. I don't see any movement from within it, which excites me. I've got my fingers crossed that it's a girl, a dead one, because Preston Druse is the closest hospital, so that's where she'd be taken. The morgue has been strangely devoid of fuckable females lately, and with the catastrophic bombshell that's just been dropped on me, I could really use a good lay. I want to see if it is, in fact, a fuckable dead girl, because I'll be able to sleep much easier if I know I've got that waiting for me tonight.

I get out of my car and look behind me, listening for any approaching vehicles. Not hearing anything but birds and the faint drone of an airplane high overhead, I cautiously approach the smoking Ford. The windshield is broken and my feet crunch over the glass scattered on the dew-moist ground.

My heart jumps when I peek inside—it *is* a girl. It's hard to make out her features because she's slumped against the steering wheel—she's not wearing her seatbelt, and the airbag failed to go off—but she's thin and athletic-looking, which is more than good enough. There's blood all over the dashboard, and I'm pretty sure she's dead.

I try to open the door so I can look at her face, but it falls off as soon as I pull on it. Cheap American-made cars. I poke her arm, and she doesn't move. I'm giddy with excitement. When I grab her shoulders to pull her back, though, she stirs and starts to cough. A mist of blood sprays onto the steering wheel. She turns her head to look at me, slowly, and her face is pretty fucked up—cuts, gashes, smears of gore, some missing front teeth, strands of her long auburn hair glued to her forehead and cheeks with matted blood.

"I'm . . . not . . . okay," she whispers. She tries to move, but cries out in pain, and tears begin to run tracks down her mashed-up face. Broken ribs, I'd imagine.

"Help," she whines. "I can't . . . it hurts . . . I'm . . . it's so . . . "

I just stand there for a few moments. I'd been counting on her being dead. I look both ways down the road again. There's still no one coming. I could go back to my car and drive off, and no one would ever know. I'm by no means *obligated* to help her.

One of the gashes on her forehead is bleeding rather profusely. If I leave, she'll probably die, unless someone else comes along in the next fifteen minutes, or so—tops, by the look of her injuries. She's breathing irregularly, with strenuous effort, and it's largely possible that one of her ribs has punctured a lung.

"Hold still," I tell her. "Try not to move." Before I even know what I'm doing, I'm unbuttoning my shirt and balling it up. I lean over and press it against her forehead, feeling it dampen immediately. With my free hand I take out my cell phone and dial 9-1-1.

My shirt soaks through in a short matter of minutes, so I drop it into the grass and peel off my undershirt and use that in its stead.

The girl's head is lolling and her breath is becoming slower. I don't know why I'm doing this. I can leave her to die, and then fuck her tonight. I have no reason at all to try to save her. I'm disgusted with myself, but I keep holding the shirt against her forehead. Soon, I can hear the peal of sirens in the distance.

"Thank you," the girl utters, barely audible. "Thank you."

I can't think of anything to say.

The ambulance pulls up, with a fire truck and two police cruisers in tow. One of the paramedics that gets out is the guy who'd been talking to me and the janitor a while back. I pray to something I don't believe in that he won't recognize me, but if anything is out there, it doesn't listen.

As the other three delicately pull the girl out of the car, and I stand there holding my blood-sopping shirt, the paramedic says to me, "Awfully kind thing for you to do, considering you made it pretty clear that you don't seem to care about who lives or dies."

"Can I go," I ask. The firemen are inspecting the car, I assume to make sure it's not going to catch fire or blow up or something. I hope it does. It would save me from having to talk to this asshole again. Now he's *really* going to remember me, and that's greatly discomforting, enough to make my stomach churn and clench with nausea.

The paramedic frowns at my flippancy. "Did you see the accident occur?"

"No. I just found her like this."

"Are you yourself hurt? Did you sustain any injuries when touching the vehicle?"

"No."

He shrugs. "You can go. I'll stop by the security office tonight and let you know how she is."

I blink at him. "Please don't," I say.

He snorts and shakes his head. "Whatever, dude. Thanks for helping out, anyway."

I pick up my other ruined shirt and walk away. I'm almost to my car when I turn around and say to the paramedic, who's about to climb into the ambulance, "Wait."

He looks over at me and raises his eyebrows. His face is hard and impatient.

"On second thought," I say, "let me know. Let me know if she makes it."

His face softens a little. "Yeah, man," he answers. "Sure, no problem."

We stand there for a moment, and then I get in my car and drive away. The girl's blood is on my hand and I get it on my steering wheel.

When I get home, I don't wipe it off.

She's not in the morgue that night.

Toward the end of my shift, the paramedic knocks on my door, and I open it. I know what he's there to tell me.

"Hey," he says, looking uncomfortable. He doesn't like talking to me; I think I creep him out, which is good. I don't want to leave any sort of impression on people, whatsoever, but I'd at least rather it be a bad one than a good one. At least that way they'll leave me alone.

"Did she make it," I ask, already knowing the answer.

"Yeah," the guy says, "we had to get her right into surgery, and the doctors said she's got a long recovery ahead of her, but she's going to be okay."

"That's really . . . tremendous," I say, figuring that's an appropriate human word for the scenario.

"She wouldn't have lived if you hadn't been there, you know. I can pretty much guarantee that."

"Okay."

"Um . . . well, yeah. Anyway, what's your name? The docs want to tell her who her savior was when she wakes up."

I cringe at that word. "No," I say. "Please . . . I . . . I don't want any recognition."

The guy gives me a weird look I can't decipher and

says, "Right, okay. Whatever, dude . . . I'll tell her it was her Friendly Neighborhood Spider-Man, or something."

"Great. You do that. Just don't give her my name."

"I don't even *know* your name, bro. Chill."

"I really don't want her to know who I am. I really don't want . . . recognition."

"Dude, I get it, it's fine. Listen, I gotta go. Thanks again, on her behalf."

"Okay."

He makes another strange face, mutters goodnight, and walks away. I close the door and lock it, sitting back down to look at the monitors.

I can't sleep.

It's been four days, I think, since I slept. *Actually* slept, I mean; I have periods where my mind kind of lapses and shuts off, while my body keeps going. Last night, or maybe two nights ago, or tonight, I was having a bored and awkward conversation with the janitor around two AM, and then, all of a sudden, I'm in the morgue, balls-deep in a dead girl's asshole, and it's just past midnight.

I don't even like anal.

Things like that keep happening. It's like time travel, almost, except some of the things that happen in the future—or the present or the past or however you want to look at it—never end up happening after I travel backward. Or maybe they do, just during one of my brain-lapse zombie moments. Maybe I'm imagining all of it. Maybe I've been kidnapped by toilet-plunger-shaped aliens from the planet Tralfamadore.

Maybe I'm dead.

I've been chugging Red Bull and averaging three pots of coffee per night, just so I can remain somewhat alert and capable of motion. Coffee makes me nauseous, and I fucking hate Red Bull.

Everything is just a means to an inevitable end that never comes soon enough.

I'm not sure how long the insomnia thing lasts. Toward the end I start seeing shit that isn't there, and *not* seeing shit that *is* there. I shouldn't drive, but I do. I think I do, at least. I always make it home to sit in my studio apartment and stare at the TV, watching-but-not-watching infomercials and daytime soap operas, and then I always make it back here to the hospital, but I have no memory of how I get to and from either place.

I haven't been going to class. My grades are high enough that they won't suffer too much from my absence, and I wouldn't be any use there, anyway. It's still early in the semester, though, and I can't afford to miss much more.

I've at least been conscious enough to avoid Helen. I haven't seen her since she told me about the pregnancy. That was when I stopped sleeping, so I can't say for sure how long it's been. Since that night, I've been locking the door to the security office, and when she knocks, I just watch her on the monitors as she stands there waiting, until she walks dejectedly away and I can breathe again.

I don't know how to face her. She's pregnant with my fucking child. *My child.* A living thing, borne from my loins. For a few days I think seriously about quitting my job, but the dead girls in the morgue win out every time. I might be an expecting father, but I still have priorities.

One night, she leaves me a note on a Post-It, stuck to the office door. All it says is, "It doesn't have to be like this." The letters are careful and rigid. I crumple up the note and shove it in my pocket.

Once I get home (again, by unknown means) I lie on my mattress and start playing Solitaire in my head. People who have been dead for a long time come into my apartment and talk to me about things I can't remember once they leave. Sometimes whole groups of them come in together, and they all talk at once, and it's distracting, so I keep losing at Solitaire.

Night comes and I remember I'm off for the next three nights, and I decide that I need to sleep. I can't keep doing this. My mind is eating away at itself (*and the mind is a terrible thing to taste . . . track four . . . track four . . . track four*). I have to sleep. I have to sleep. If I don't sleep, I'll go crazy.

I've mentioned before that I don't drink. I hate the taste of it, and the way it makes me feel. But I have to sleep, and I know alcohol makes people pass out, and I live above a fucking bar, for fuck's sake, so I might as well change things up a little.

I go downstairs and into the Bad Seed and sit at the bar. The bartender, who's also the owner, who's also my landlord, is an old junkie named Nick, who has a habit of shooting up right in front of his patrons. They don't mind because they're usually doing something similar. "The divest dive bar in the Cleveland area", they call this place. The smell of cigarette smoke isn't enough to cover up the stench of sweat and sex and puke, and I'm reminded of why I don't ever come down here.

Nick is leaning against the bar, smoking a joint, looking pale and sick and wasted, and writing something in a notebook. He told me once that he wrote a novel, even got it published. Something about a dead rabbit, I think. He's a musician, too, and he swears he's the best lyricist since John Lennon. Whatever, I don't listen to the Beatles.

He looks up and smiles at me when I sit down. "Hey there, kid. This is a neat surprise," he says, putting his notebook down and wiping some drool from his chin with the back of his white hand. "I didn't figure you for a drinker."

"I'm not," I say. "But I am tonight."

"That's what I say every night," he says with a wheezy chuckle. He coughs into the track-marked crook of his arm and asks, "What'll you have, boy-o? First round is on me."

"I don't care," I say, lighting a cigarette and moving a nearby ashtray closer to me. It's shaped like a heart, which I find odd and out-of-place. "Whatever will get me drunk the fastest."

He chuckles again. "Well, how's about I fix you up my specialty drink? I call it 'the Wild Rose', after *the* Wild Rose, owner and namesake of the most glorious adult entertainment club in the US."

The Wild Rose is a strip club down the street. I've never been to a strip club. They don't have any dead girls there.

"That's fine," I say. "It doesn't matter."

Nick turns around and starts making the drink. "You know, Rose and I were a hot little item, back in the day," he says. "Shit, I could tell you some stories about the pussy on that girl. Hey, did you pay your rent this month?"

"Yeah. I gave it to you last week." He does this a lot.

He shrugs and puts the drink in front of me, on top of a little square napkin that appears to have been used for the expulsion of snot from his or someone else's nose. "Okay, I trust you," he says, leaning back and lighting another joint. "Sorry, I tend to be forgetful sometimes."

"It's fine."

"I think it's the drugs," he says.

"It's understandable." I look down at the drink. It's dark, and there's no ice in it. I take a deep breath and down it in two laborious swallows. I put the glass down and cough breathlessly into my hand. My throat and nose and chest burn, and I'm thinking maybe I should have just taken a handful of Benadryl in the interest of passing out, as opposed to subjecting myself to this, but I don't like taking pills.

Helen.

Helen and her dead eyes.

Helen with my baby inside her.

"Get me another one," I say.

"You got it, champ. You want to buy some blow?"

"No. Just the drink is fine."

He shrugs again and goes about mixing the drink. The bar door opens with an accompanying sound of a tinkling bell, and a man in a business suit staggers in, maybe forty-ish, his tie hanging loosely from his neck, and his sweaty hair disheveled. He sits on the stool beside me, even though the rest of the bar is open, and now I'm *really* wishing I'd just bought some fucking Benadryl.

"I think my wife is cheating on me," he says, and then tells Nick to get him a strawberry cheesecake martini. Beneath the reek of alcohol and cigarettes, there's a scent of expensive aftershave and cologne.

"What the fuck is a strawberry cheesecake martini?" Nick asks, sliding me my drink and regarding the guy in the suit with a disgusted look on his face. "This is the *Bad Seed*, man. If you want some pansy drink, there's all kinds of places down the street that you can go to. I don't even know how to make a *regular* fucking martini."

"I've been barhopping along this street all night, and I keep getting kicked out," the man says. "For fighting." He looks over at me.

"I'm not going to fight you," I say distractedly as I stare at the awful beverage before me, trying to gather the will to drink it.

"Just get me a stout, then," the man tells Nick. "I should probably cool it on the hard liquor, anyway."

When Nick walks over to the tap to fill the glass, the man turns to me and says again, "I think my wife is cheating on me."

"That's really tragic," I say, reaching for my drink and then retracting my hand so I can clutch the edge of the bar to prevent myself from tumbling off the stool. The effects of the first drink are starting to set in and mix unpleasantly with my exhaustion. Instead of wanting to sleep, I just want to fall over and look up at the cracks in the ceiling and wish I was dead.

"Yeah, dude, it *is* fucking tragic," he says. Nick brings him the beer, and he takes a big gulp. He wipes foam from his lip with the back of his hand and glares at me.

I'm not really looking at him; I'm still staring at my drink, and I tell him again, "I'm not going to fight you."

"I travel a lot," he continues. "Like, all the time. I'm usually only home for a day or two at a time before I have to leave again. Yeah, she's probably lonely, or whatever, but that doesn't give her an excuse to go and fuck someone else, you know? And, I mean, sure, sometimes I engage in a little, uh, extracurricular activity, but it's usually when I'm in another country, so it doesn't count, right?" He takes another big swig of his beer and belches.

"Sure," I say. I blink rapidly, trying to stop the world from spinning. Maybe this is what they call "being a lightweight". I don't know how people do this all the time.

"And, for Christ's sake, I'm an international *businessman*, goddammit. I'm *stressed* and under a lot of *pressure*. I have *needs*. It's different for men, especially men like me. I have an excuse. She doesn't."

"Right," I say. "Definitely." I take a tentative sip of the cocktail and cough again. The man asks me for a cigarette, and I hand him one.

"Who smokes Lucky Strikes anymore?" he asks, putting it in his mouth and lighting it with a fancy Zippo that's engraved with something I can't make out.

"I do," I say.

"You know," he goes on, exhaling loudly through his mouth, "she hasn't been wearing her wedding ring lately. Like, what the fuck is up with that, right? She says it's 'because of her job,' or whatever, but I think that's bullshit. And fuck, I can't even *remember* the last time we had sex. When I come home, she barely even acknowledges me."

"That's awful," I say, and then lift my glass to my lips but decide I'm not ready for another mouthful of napalm, so I set it back down.

"I think I'm losing her, man," the guy says, suddenly turning sullen. His face turns down, and I think there are tears in his eyes. "What the hell am I supposed to do?"

After a few moments, I realize he's looking at me expectantly, anticipating a response. I say, "I don't know. Buy her something." That's what Americans do, right? They buy shit. I have no way of knowing if it works, but that's what they do, and it's the best answer I have.

The man nods slowly, contemplating this. "Yeah," he says. "That's not a bad idea. She really needs a new car. I think she's got a lemon or something. It's a great car, but it's a piece of shit."

"Sorry to hear that." *Please, please, leave me the fuck alone.*

"Then again," he says, "I don't know if I want to go through all the hassle of buying a car, you know what I'm saying? It's such a pain in the fucking ass."

I wouldn't know. I've never bought a car; the Toyota was my mother's, and one of the many things left to me upon her death. "Buy her flowers," I say, thinking of the tiger lilies I'd bought for Helen. I wonder if they're still in the vase on her table. I wonder why I care. I force myself to take another sip.

"Flowers, yeah, now *there's* a fuckin' good idea," he replies, nodding more vigorously, smiling a little. He claps me on the back and says, "Thanks, dude, you're a real fuckin' pal. You don't meet a whole lot of good guys anymore. Nice to know there's still decent folks out there. Your next round is on me."

"I'm not going to have another round," I tell him, feeling my forehead begin to perspire.

I think you're a good guy, you know, Helen had told me.

A real fuckin' pal, according to Mr. Sleazy Businessman.

I'm covered in sweat. I have to get out of here.

I stand unsteadily and toss a twenty on the bar and mutter something about checking the monitors. I stumble back to the stairs, dragging myself up them, and lurch into my apartment. Exhausted, so exhausted, but not sleepy.

I must sleep.

I shuffle over to the wall and place my palms against it, then proceed to bash my forehead into it with all the strength I can muster. Blood runs into my eyes, but I still keep bashing. My vision starts to blink in and out and turn gray, and finally narrows into a tunnel-like tube, and then it's all gone and all black, and I'm falling backward and slipping away, and then I'm gone.

I don't wake up until eight o' clock the next evening. I feel wonderful, almost like I do after fucking a nice fresh corpse. I stand and stretch and look outside at the autumn night's fading light. My head is clear. I can think again.

And there are things about which I must think.

Helen keeps trying to talk to me, and I keep avoiding her. One night I bump into her in the hallway, on one of my rounds, so I turn and run the other way. Another night she comes outside while I'm smoking, looks at me for a moment, and then asks for a cigarette. I stub out my own with my shoe and then go wordlessly inside. She tries to block my path, but I brush past her.

Things go on like this for a while, this pathetic game of cat and mouse, except the cat is pregnant with the mouse's baby. A month goes by, and then a second and third, and finally a fourth. It's winter, and it's cold. I get better at avoiding Helen, but I watch her on the monitors, watching as she slowly grows visibly pregnant. Some of the nurses start giddily putting their hands on her stomach. I've never understood that shit.

One night, I doze off into a light half-sleep while reading Will Self's *Umbrella* (it's a difficult and cumbersome read, even for me), and when I wake up, Helen's sitting there watching me. The slight swell of her stomach is even more disturbing up close. I can't stop staring at it. Her breasts look bigger, too, but I don't care about that. It's her stomach. Her fucking stomach, and the fucking thing inside of it.

She nods at the book in my lap. "I'm glad you're liking him," she says. "He's my favorite author."

"Yeah," I say. "Great. What do you want. How did you get in here."

"You left the door unlocked." I can tell she's hurt by my brusque callousness, and I feel a faint, unwelcome pang somewhere inside of me.

"Shit," I say. "Goddammit." I haven't been sleeping well again—in fact, I think it's been about three days since I last slept—and my wits aren't entirely about me. The insomnia hasn't gotten to the point of being unbearable ever since the bout that ended in my having to bash myself to sleep, but there are periods of time when all I can think about is the impending birth of my child, and sleep becomes an impossibility for a few days.

"Are you really that dead-set against talking to me?" Helen asks, still looking upset.

"Yeah," I say. "You should go."

"No," she answers, suddenly becoming indignant. "This is ridiculous. You're the father of my—"

"Stop it. Don't say shit like that. It makes me want to throw up. Jesus, Helen. You eat babies. You eat them. You don't have them."

"Like I said, it's different this time. It's *mine*, and it's *special*."

"You need to kill it."

"No."

"It's really a simple procedure, you know. They just let the air in."

She glares at me, but cracks a small half-smile. "Are you *actually* quoting *Hemingway* right now?"

"It's true," I say, kind of impressed she caught the reference. "It's very simple."

"I'm a maternity doctor, in case you forgot. I know how it works. Besides, it's too late anyway. I'm too far along into the pregnancy." She sighs, and then smiles again. "I know what it is. You don't like fat girls. You don't want to watch me get fat and turn into a big white elephant."

"That really isn't funny."

"You started it."

"Why are you here," I ask again.

She lowers her gaze to her bloated stomach and rubs it lovingly. "We *have* something," she says. "Don't you get that? It's not just this baby—we had something before that. We're the same. You're the only person I can relate to. And . . . I miss you."

Excuse me while I go puke and then commit *hara kari* with a tree branch, or something. I can't handle sentimentality. I really, really can't.

And then, as if she can see right into my fucked-up head, she says, "Okay, I'm sorry, I know you don't like that kind of thing. But . . . it's true. And even though sometimes it seems like all you're doing is tolerating me . . . I know you at least *sort of* enjoy my company. I mean, you *did* go on a date with me." She smiles at this.

I frown. "Yeah. I'm really not sure why I did that."

"You *fucked* me."

"Not really sure why I did that, either."

She sighs again, rubs her stomach again. "Either way, you *did*. There's *something* there, I know there is. You feel something for me."

"I don't really know how to feel anything."

"You don't know how to, but you do. For me, you do."

I can't think of anything to say.

"Stop locking the door, okay? Please? I won't . . . I won't come around and bother you as much, but there's no reason for you to shun me like this."

"Abort the baby and you can come see me as much as you want."

She shakes her head and stands up. "I have to go," she says. "Please stop locking the door."

I don't say anything.

She purses her lips, sighs a third time, and leaves. I lock the door behind her.

A couple of days later, Nick comes up to my apartment around noon to get the rent. I hand it to him in a rolled-up wad of bills that he flattens out and counts right there in front of me, even though I've lived here for five years and never once have I shorted him. I suspect it's a junkie thing.

"Thanks, kid," he tells me, and I'm about to shut the door when he stops me and says, "Hey, wait, I almost forgot—that guy was down at the bar last night. He wanted me to thank you for him."

"What guy," I ask. "Thank me for what."

"You know," he says. "That one guy. The one who came in when you were down there that one night. It was . . . I don't know, a while ago. Whenever it was, he came in and told us that he thought his wife was cheating on him."

Shit. That guy. The one I'd accidentally advised on

how to repair his marriage. He'd remembered me, just as I'd feared. My presence had become tangible to yet another human being, so much so that four or five months—or however long it had been—hadn't been long enough for the memory of that conversation to fade away. He'd been pretty wasted, too, so the fact that he remembered anything at all from that night is startling, in and of itself. "What did he say," I ask weakly, not really wanting to know.

"He said he got his wife flowers, just like you told him to, and that it worked. They . . . fucked, I guess. And apparently now they've got a kid on the way. He said you saved his marriage *and* helped him start a family, all with just a little friendly advice."

"That sounds a little . . . extreme," I say. "I'm sure he was . . . exaggerating."

Nick waves his hand dismissively. He almost drops the wad of cash, so he hastily jams it in his back pocket, looking flustered. "No, man, he was pretty adamant. He wasn't even drunk, either. Said he's gonna make a habit of getting her flowers every time he comes into town from one of his trips, in the hopes it'll get him laid." Nick snickers at this for some reason.

"Okay," I say. "I really have to go."

He shrugs, pats his back pocket to make sure the money is still there, and then goes down the stairs. I shut my door and bolt all six locks.

What is happening to me.

I'm saving lives, saving marriages, and helping start families, for fuck's sake.

At that last part I think of Helen, Helen and our baby, Helen and *our* fucked-up little family. Is that what we'll call it? A *family*? Will she ask me to move in? Will I say yes?

No.

I would say no.

At least, that's what I like to think.

I also would have liked to think that I'd let that girl in the park die, though.

I light a cigarette and peek out my curtains, peering through the blinds, looking at the harsh light of the day, the empty sidewalks, and the pothole-pocked road. Jubilee Street is ugly during the day; its aesthetic appeal, if you could call it that, is dependent on a darkness pierced only by headlights and neon and the glow of lit cigarettes.

Everything is prettier in the dark.

I close the curtains and turn off the lights, sitting against the wall and smoking. I wonder if I could arrange for Helen to accidentally fall down some stairs, or something. Not in the interest of seriously hurting her, because I don't want that—I really am a peaceful creature, and I still do sort of like her, even though she's carrying life I helped create. No, I really don't want to hurt her too badly—just enough so the thing inside of her dies.

I wonder how she'd react if I punched her in the stomach.

I wonder if I even possess the physical strength to do enough damage.

Jesus, when did my life become so fucked up.

I stop locking the security room door.

As promised, she doesn't come around as much, but a couple of times a week she'll show up and tell me her dreams, or ask me about my sex life with the dead, which hasn't been very active lately; I can't seem to concentrate, and I've been having difficulty . . . getting it up. There was a gorgeous college cheerleader in here the other night, who had broken her neck when she'd fallen from the top of one of those human pyramid things they do. It was a big thing in the news, and it had happened on live television, so I got to watch the video and jack off to it. But when she'd been here, waiting for me in the morgue, I'd stood before her goddess-like body and been completely unable to perform.

It was Helen's fault, I think; she'd visited me earlier that night, and she hadn't been wearing her long white coat, so her belly was more visible, and more bloated than ever. Sickeningly so. She's almost six months pregnant, now. I don't even think back alley abortion doctors will so much as *consider* sticking a coat hanger up there at this point.

Meanwhile, Helen is changing in more ways than her fattening stomach. She tells me she's becoming more and more apathetic, that she's having all these weird dreams and they're making her think a lot, think about how people are in comparison to how she is. She tells me normal life is becoming less and less attractive to her.

She tells me she's not going to raise our baby to be normal.

We're in the morgue when she tells me this. She's come with me to help me look for a suitable girl to fuck, convinced she'll be able to help me get hard. I'm really just humoring her at this point, because she's been harassing me to let her help for over a week now. The two of us walk around lifting up the sheets, not having any luck. Most of them are men, and the few women are either fat and ugly or fat, *old*, and ugly. I've fucked dead old women before, but they have to be in moderately decent shape, and I have to be pretty desperate.

I'm really not that desperate right now.

Not for a fuck, at least.

My mind is otherwise occupied.

For the most part, Helen at least respects my wishes and doesn't talk about the baby. But tonight, she's been trying to get my input on a name for it, because she now knows it's a girl, and she's very excited about this—too excited for me to get her to shut up about it.

"I'm not seeing anyone good enough," I say, putting the sheet back over some dead kid and sitting against the wall to light a cigarette.

"I'm not, either," Helen says, and comes over to sit by me. She has to be careful when she sits down.

With her next to me like this, I could probably elbow her hard enough in the stomach to be potentially harmful to the thing inside. I hand her a cigarette, instead, and light it for her.

"I really want a *unique* name for her, you know?" she says, lazily blowing smoke into the cold air. "I want her name to be unique because *she* is going to be unique. Unique as in, fucked up. Fucked up like me. Like *us*."

"What are you talking about," I ask. I loathe

conversations about the little fucking brat, but this is particularly unnerving.

"I'm not sure yet, exactly," she says dreamily. "But I don't want her to be normal. At all. I know that for sure now. I've thought about it a lot. I've *dreamt* about it a lot. Last night, I had a dream that, for her thirteenth birthday, I took her to an abortion clinic and cut one of the fetuses in half, and we shared it."

"That's pretty fucked up, Helen." And this is coming from me.

She beams and blows smoke in my face. "*Exactly*. Perfectly, wonderfully fucked up, and in such a poetic way. I was thirteen when I ate my first baby."

"You also had a ferret that ate your brother when you were six."

Her face darkens. "I've been thinking about that, too, and I'm not entirely sure that's related. I think maybe I was just born with a taste for babies."

"Are you hearing what you're saying."

"Maybe it won't be babies, though," she says, not hearing me. "Maybe she'll have some other little quirk." Her stoned eyes are alight with wistful wonderings as she thinks about the endless possibilities for her—*our*—fucked up child.

"Jesus, Helen," I say, lighting another cigarette with the burning butt of my last one. "The things we do—they're not quirks."

She's still not listening. "Maybe she'll . . . maybe she'll be a killer," she muses. "Could you imagine if our daughter was a serial killer?"

"Helen," I say, "what the fuck has happened to you."

She looks deeply at me with an expression that's

far too affectionate and says, "You, darling. *You* happened to me."

She actually reaches up and strokes my stubbly cheek. I angrily brush it away and say, "Don't call me darling."

The next night, when we're outside smoking in the frigid winter air, Helen tells me she killed someone last night. She's smiling when she says it.

I really don't know how to respond to something like that. I think about it for a second, sucking on my cigarette, and then say quietly, "Um . . . were you . . . naked when you did it."

She cocks her head and squints at me through the smoke. "Why would I be naked?" she asks.

"Because you're naked when you eat babies." I'm thinking back to how I met her, finding her sitting in the morgue with a half-devoured infant corpse in her hands, and how all I could say was, "Why are you naked."

"I wasn't naked," she says. She's standing there, smoking and looking at me, waiting for a reaction, which is irritating because she should know by now that I really don't do reactions. She has her free hand pressed lightly, almost protectively, against her stomach. That's another thing I've never understood about pregnant women. It's like they're trying to hold the baby in, for fear it might come tumbling out.

I wish it would.

I wish it would fall right out onto the pavement so I could squash the fucking thing.

"I killed someone," Helen says again. Her expression is peculiar, and I can't read it. I'm really not sure how a person would feel after killing someone. Especially not a person like her. Or me.

Could I kill someone?

Am I capable of it?

Could I kill Helen and sufficiently end the pregnancy debacle, cutting it off at the source? I could get away with it, I'm sure—I'm smart, and I'd figure something out.

But could I actually do it?

And—*Helen*, of all people—could I really kill *her*?

Do I really even want to?

"I *killed* someone," Helen says for a third time, and she's smiling again. Her eyes dart around to make sure we're alone. She looks over her shoulder and then back at me and says, "A *person*. One of the *normal people*. I *killed* her."

"I don't understand," I say. None of this feels real. I'm standing outside smoking with a baby-eating maternity doctor, who's carrying my child, and she is now proudly proclaiming to me that she's recently become a murderer.

"What don't you understand?" She flicks the cigarette away and holds both hands to the bloated stomach beneath her coat.

"How," I ask. "How did you do it. Why did you do it."

"She was dying, right there in front of me," she says, almost giddily. She takes a step closer to me and lowers her voice. "The baby was fine, which is unfortunate, but that's not the point. The mother— she was bleeding out. *Technically,* I did everything I was *supposed* to do to try and save her. *But*—here's the thing—I saw a way. I won't bore you with all the medical terminology, and procedures that you wouldn't understand anyway, but . . . I could have saved her. I saw something that none of the other doctors or nurses saw, and I could have stopped the bleeding. The woman could have lived."

She's grinning from ear to ear, and in this moment, her beauty has become, in some abstract sense, nightmarish.

"But I let her die," she says.

"Why," I ask. My hands are shaking for some reason. My legs feel weak. I drop the cigarette and lean against the building.

Helen's smile turns downward. "What do you mean? I had the opportunity, so I took it. I thought you'd be proud of me, or something."

"I don't kill people, Helen. I fuck dead girls."

Her frown turns further downward. "I told you, I'm seeing things differently. I'm seeing *people* differently. I keep thinking, fuck everyone, it's just me and my baby." She pauses. "*Our* baby," she says, "if you want it to be."

"Don't."

She sighs and turns away and walks out from under the awning to look up at the star-spangled sky. A light snow has begun to fall. I think about following her, but only for a moment. I'm about to go back inside when she turns and says to me, "I am what I am. I'm coming to terms with that. I was looking down at this woman, this woman who was dying, and I thought, what would she think of me, if she knew what I was?"

"What does it matter."

"It *doesn't* matter," she says, smiling again. "And *she* doesn't matter, either. I keep thinking about the things you've said, about normalcy and normal people. I keep thinking about how you *see* things. And . . . it's easier to think like that, to see things like you do. It's so . . . *liberating*. I thought of all that, and I thought, why should this woman live? So, I let her die. In essence, I *killed* her. I thought you'd be impressed. I mean, if you had a chance to kill someone, someone *normal*, and get away with it, wouldn't you?"

I look at her stomach and think again about killing her, musing on the idea for a second, but that wasn't her question. "I don't think so," I say. "I'm too apathetic to kill people. They're not worth the effort. And when you kill someone, you become the most important thing about that person's life. I don't want to be important to anyone."

She gently rubs her stomach. "You're important to *me*," she says.

"Don't," I say again. "Please." The soft tone of her voice grinds at me, like a snow shovel scraping a driveway. I glance at the security camera overhead and think, for a brief second, that if it weren't there I might run over and shove her down and punch her in the stomach until blood started to seep from between her legs. Then I wince at the thought, urgently pushing it away. I'm really not a violent person.

Just a desperate one.

"The woman," Helen says. "The woman I killed . . . she's in the morgue. She's all yours."

I put a cigarette in my mouth, raise my lighter, then decide that I don't want it and put it back in the pack. "I'm not in the mood," I tell her. I pocket the pack of cigarettes and say, "Listen, I have to go ch—"

"Don't say it," Helen says. "Don't even say it."

I blink at her, a little confused, and then I nod and say, "Okay." I leave her there and go inside.

She comes by a couple of more times after that, but we don't talk much. Then she disappears. She doesn't come in to the hospital at all. I flip through all the monitors for her, every night, but she's not there.

After she's been missing for a week and a half, I'm sitting in the security office around midnight when my cell phone rings.

My cell phone never rings.

Seriously, *never*.

I flip it open warily and the caller ID says it's Helen.

I don't remember giving her my number.

I have hers, but she shouldn't have mine.

I answer it. I don't say anything in greeting; I just press the ACCEPT button and wait for her to start talking.

"Are you there?" she whispers from the other end, after a moment of silence.

"Yeah," I say. "How did you get my number."

There's some rustling, and then a noise that sounds like she's blowing her nose, and then nothing.

"Helen," I say. "What's going on."

"It's dead."

"What's dead."

"She is. She's dead inside me." There's a barked sobbing noise, and then she blows her nose again.

"That . . . sucks," I say. When she doesn't answer, I think that maybe this wasn't the best response, so I follow it up with, "Do you know for sure. Do you know for sure that it's dead."

"What the fuck kind of question is that? How the fuck would I *not* know? I'm a fucking maternity doctor, for fuck's sake."

"Yeah," I capitulate. "That makes sense." This is one of those rare situations where it's convenient that I'm principally unable to express emotion, because I'm feeling rather gleeful at this revelation. That fucking baby represented an all-inclusive end to my life, and not in the attractive sense, i.e. death. My existence would have been ruined. She had claimed she wouldn't demand any responsibility on my part, but she and I both knew it wouldn't end up working that way.

But *now* . . . now it doesn't matter.

Now it's *dead*, and I am once again *free*.

"I need you," Helen says. "I need you to come over."

"I'm at work, Helen."

"Leave."

I sigh. I *could* radio the janitor and have him keep an eye on things—tell him I've become violently ill with some sort of stomach virus, or something. I've never once missed a day of work, so I don't think it would be too big of a deal.

The problem, though, is that I don't *want* to go over to Helen's.

I'm not emotionally equipped to even *remotely* be

able to comfort a grieving woman who's just suffered a miscarriage.

I *am*, however, in a delightfully good mood. Death in general gets me pretty excited, especially the death of children, and more than anything, of course, the death of *my* child, that I had never wanted.

I guess I'm just feeling kind of generous, or something. I tell Helen, after another sigh (this one simply for dramatic effect), "Fine, I'll see what I can do."

"Thank you," she says, but it's not gratitude in her voice—it's despair. At least, I think it is. It's hard enough for me to figure out people's emotions when I'm face to face with them; it's another thing, entirely, when it's over the phone.

"Give me half an hour, I guess," I tell her, and then hang up before she can say anything else.

I park on the street, walk up the driveway, and ring the doorbell. I'm holding a bouquet of cheap yellow roses I picked up from an all-night convenience store on the way over. I thought a miscarriage probably warrants flowers just as much as a first date does.

When she doesn't answer, I ring it again, wait a minute or so, and then knock. When she still doesn't answer, I try the door handle, and it's unlocked. I figure, shit, I've been inside this woman, and watched her eat a baby, so I think that's all pretty much worthy of entry into her home.

"Helen," I call out, stepping into the foyer and closing the front door behind me, hanging my long black coat on the rack. She doesn't answer, so I walk down the hall and into the kitchen. There's already a bouquet of roses in a vase on the table, where my tiger lilies had been once upon a time. They're red and white, and far more expensive-looking than my shabby yellow ones. They're a little wilted, though, probably a couple of weeks old and nearing their death. I set my own roses on the table and go into the living room.

Seeing Helen, it's so much like the time I first met her in the morgue that, for a brief second, I wonder if I'm time traveling again, *Slaughterhouse-Five*-style. I try to remember the last time I've slept. Last night, it was last night, yes. So this is really happening.

"Why are you naked," is all I can think to say.

She's sitting on one of her sheets, legs spread out before her like she's waiting to be fucked, and maybe she is. Her stomach is round and gross. There are two empty pill bottles lying beside her, next to a gleaming surgical scalpel. I think back to the first night I saw Helen, in the delivery room with the stillborn baby and its murderous/suicidal father.

"I have to be," she says, her head lolling. There's dried drool on her chin, and her eyes have never been deader. If she wasn't sitting up and talking, I'd think she *was* dead. "I have to be naked because I'm going to make a mess. You know I'm a messy eater."

"Yeah," I say. "But what are you going to eat. There's no baby here." I look around, wondering if maybe there's a fetus in a container I hadn't noticed, but I don't see one anywhere. When she doesn't say anything, I repeat myself. "Helen, what are you going to eat."

She looks at her stomach and picks up the scalpel.

"Helen," I say, taking a step forward. "No. Don't."

"What other choice do I have?" she asks, trying to look at me, but unable to maintain an eye-locked gaze because her head keeps tipping this way and that, like it's too heavy for her neck to support. "You even said I'd just end up eating it, anyway. Besides, it's kind of poetic, don't you think?"

"No, Helen," I say, taking another step forward. "I really don't think it's very poetic."

"Don't you think I'm beautiful?"

"Yeah," I say, drawing in a deep breath, unable to discern whether I'm more upset about the scenario unfolding before me, or about the fact that I just admitted to a live woman that I think she's beautiful. She is, though, minus the fat stomach—her dead face, her golden hair splayed across her shoulders, her already-full breasts made ever-fuller by the pregnancy, nipples standing erect, the lips of her cunt seeming to whisper to me—yes, she is beautiful.

Helen smiles. "That's very sweet. I'm glad you think that."

"How is that relevant, Helen."

"Don't you remember what Poe said? About beautiful women, and death?"

I shiver a little as I recall the passage to which she's referring. "Yeah," I say quietly. "Yeah, I remember."

"Say it."

"No."

"*SAY IT!*" she bellows, startling me and making my heart skip. She's breathing heavily, her teeth bared and breasts heaving, and I feel myself start to get inexplicably hard.

I can't remember the exact wording, so I paraphrase and say quietly, "There's nothing more poetic than the death of a beautiful woman."

The vicious look on her face dissipates into one of serene contentment, and she nods, closing her eyes. "Yes," she says. "Thank you." And then she casually drags the scalpel across her bloated stomach.

"Helen," I say, falling to my knees and reaching my hand out in protest, but unable to keep my dick from rising in excitement as the blood begins to flow over the slope of her belly and down between her legs, soaking the sheet and the insides of her legs, slathering her vagina in red. "Jesus, Helen, what are you doing."

She slips her free hand into the slit across her stomach, reaching inside, and then stabs the scalpel farther into the wound, making careful cuts at whatever is within that's keeping her from her feast. "I can feel it," she says giddily. She has blood almost up to her elbows. "I can feel her. She's very, very dead."

I collapse back against the couch and can't do anything but sit there and watch as she fishes around inside of herself for our dead kid.

"It's a shame," Helen says as she sets aside the scalpel and then plunges her hand back inside her gushing stomach. "We really could have had something, you know? We could have been a happy, fucked-up little family, and it would have been great. We would have put all those normal families to shame."

"Yeah," I say, humoring her because she's dying anyway. I'm just trying to figure out how I feel about the whole situation. Seriously, I like Helen. She's the closest thing I've ever had to a friend. And *no*, I'm *not* getting sentimental. On the contrary, don't friends react a little more . . . intensely, when they watch their friends die? Especially when their friends are trying to wrench a dead baby out of their own stomach for the purpose of ingestion?

I don't know, I guess this is kind of a special circumstance.

"I've got her," Helen says, smiling wider than I've ever seen her smile. She struggles for a few more seconds and then lifts the wretched thing from within her, a red, humanoid creature, tethered to her by the thin rope of an umbilical cord.

"I'm bleeding out," Helen says weakly as she forces herself to sit up straighter. "I have to hurry." For a brief moment, she looks at the fetus with a soft expression that I think is motherly love, or something, probably imagining all it could have been, and then she lifts it to her mouth and begins to eat.

Now, we've already been through this part. The noises, the chomping, the groans, *et cetera*—so I won't go into vivid detail. Just know it's as jarring as it was the first time around. She still manages to pleasure herself as she's eating, her sexual juices mixing with the ever-running blood, sometimes squirting out in a thin pink stream, or an occasional misty spray. She eats the umbilical cord, too—gnawing on it a little and then slurping the rest up like a spaghetti noodle.

My dick could cut through diamonds right now.

I've unzipped my jeans, and I'm stroking myself as I watch her.

Finally, once she's . . . I don't know, *full*, I guess, she tosses aside what little remains of the fetus and looks at me. She's completely covered in gore, from her face to her feet, and she's shuddering with what I think is probably a combination of pleasure and blood loss.

She reeks of the death smell.

"Fuck me," she says. "Fuck me as I'm dying."

"No," I say. "Not until you're dead."

Now is the part where I'm supposed to say something meaningful to her as the last wisps of life begin to drift from her. I'm supposed to, I don't know, utter some long-winded soliloquy about our relationship, about all she did for me, or whatever. Maybe we would even kiss, and cry, and I'd hold her until I felt her breathing cease and her heart chug slowly to a final halt. I would delicately close her eyes and—

Blah, blah, blah, go fuck yourself. If you're looking for that kind of shit, go read a LaVyrle Spencer novel.

That kind of shit doesn't happen in my world.

Nope. I just silently watch her die.

Once I tell her I'm not going to fuck her until she's dead, she must not have the energy to argue because she just lets herself fall onto her back and lie there. I wait until the rise and fall of her breasts stops, and the blood no longer pulses from her stomach, and then I get up.

I drop my pants.

I step toward her, out of my jeans, peeling off my shirt as I go, and then . . .

I mount.

She's still warm, but that's okay. She's *dead*. There's the baby weight issue, the flabby skin left behind from her stretched stomach, but that's okay, too. I can look past that, because she is dead, and she is wonderful. She lies there, limply flopping a little as I fuck the living daylights (er, you know what I mean) out of her, and she is sex incarnate. I smack her dead tits around. I yank so hard on her hair that golden handfuls come out in my fists. I kiss her dead, bloody mouth and my tongue picks up flecks of fetus.

Next, I decide to skull-fuck her, which is something I've always wanted to do. I jam my fingers into her eye and pluck out the eyeball, squeezing it in my fist and loving the feeling of its juices running down my forearm. Then, gently, I lift her head and insert my cock into the empty socket, thrusting in and out, feeling her brains churn around inside her head.

Bear with me, it's almost over.

When the skull-fucking gets boring, I pull out of her eye socket and go back to fucking her dead cunt, shrieking and hooting and hollering like a crazed, maniacal barbarian. There's so much blood everywhere, and it's all just so fucking funny.

Just as I'm about to come, I belt out a yodeling howl (think of Tarzan swinging on a vine) and bury my hands inside her. Shoving my arms in up to the elbows and squishing her dead organs, pulling some of them out and pitching them at the wall, tugging out coils of her intestines and rubbing them over my body, and then I absolutely fucking *explode* inside of her. It's the purest orgasm any man ever felt in the history of sex—I lift out from my body and am sucked into space, my entire being shattering into individual chunks of ecstasy, and every god there ever was bows down to my carnal supremacy, and then there's only light and it is a *good* light, I am not afraid of it, and it consumes me and then I'm back in Helen's house, falling off her, covered in her blood and intestines, and I'm laughing—I'm not sure if I've ever laughed in my life, *really* laughed, but oh, I'm laughing now, and I feel better than I thought was possible. I look at my dick and it's still spurting out intermittent spouts of residual semen, and my abdominal muscles are clenching ever tighter with the most exquisite bliss known to man.

After a while, I stand and look around at the mess. I run a bloody hand through my hair, which has gotten kind of long, and for a few seconds I think about perhaps getting a haircut tomorrow.

Deciding I should probably clean myself up, I find Helen's bathroom upstairs and step into the shower, letting the hot water run over me for I don't know how long. I think about what's just happened, how glorious I feel, how my life will never be the same again. I have no idea how I'll be able to equal or surpass the pleasure I just experienced, and I wonder if I've reached the absolute highest peak in my life. Whether the only way to go is down, and this is a little dismaying but I don't care right now. I just smile, *really* smile, and let the water run over me.

As Helen washes off me and swirls around the drain and gets slurped into the penetralia of the sewers, I guess I feel something. I don't know what, but something.

When the shower finally turns cold, I shut off the

nozzle, towel myself off, and walk downstairs, naked. I stretch in front of the picture window and look out at the night. The arrogant grin of the moon is high, and its palace of stars gleams bright. The rest is darkness, and it is good.

And then, the darkness is penetrated. *Violated.*

Raped by two bold yellow lights drawing closer to the house.

Headlights coming up the driveway.

Scratching my head, I back away from the window and stand looking at the door, listening to the sound of the car outside. I look over my shoulder at the wilted roses in the vase on the kitchen table, and suddenly a lot of things start to piece together and make sense.

Me and . . . I haven't had sex in a long time.

My . . . someone was able to fix it for me.

She really needs a new car. I think she's got a lemon or something. It's a great car, but it's a piece of shit.

He said he got his wife flowers, just like you told him to, and that it worked. They . . . fucked, I guess. And apparently now they've got a kid on the way.

A montage of all the little things I'd ignored, all flashing through my head to the accompaniment of the *Saw* theme music that plays whenever the plot twist is revealed at the end of each movie.

I sigh and think, *Well, shit. This sucks.*

I hear the car engine shut off.

I walk back to the living room and pick up my discarded shirt, taking my cigarettes out of the pocket and lighting one. I sit on the couch and look at the savage, grisly scene before me, and I try to think of how someone normal would react to it.

I guess I'm about to find out.

I hear the door open.

I hear someone come inside.

I hear a man's voice call out, "Helen? I'm home, and I brought you flowers again, so I'm expecting to get some tonight!"

I smirk as I smoke.

I hope he likes sloppy seconds.

About the Author

Little is known about Chandler's origins. He has claimed, on separate occasions, to be both from Helltown, California, and Cleveland, Ohio. To date, it is still unclear from which locale he actually hails. He currently resides in Los Angeles, but sightings of him are rare. He is the author of *Until the Sun, Just to See Hell*, and *Hate to Feel*.